ELEANOR

ELEANOR

---

*She never expected
Deceit, Lies & Suspense in a Small Town*

Charlotte Lewis

Charlotte Lewis

Copyright © 2007 by Charlotte Lewis.

ISBN 10:   Softcover   1-4257-4780-9

ISBN 13:   Softcover   978-1-4257-4780-0

All rights reserved. No part of this book may be reproduced or transmitted in any form or by any means, electronic or mechanical, including photocopying, recording, or by any information storage and retrieval system, without permission in writing from the copyright owner.

This is a work of fiction. Names, characters, places and incidents either are the product of the author's imagination or are used fictitiously, and any resemblance to any actual persons, living or dead, events, or locales is entirely coincidental.

This book was printed in the United States of America.

To order additional copies of this book, contact:
Xlibris Corporation
1-888-795-4274
www.Xlibris.com
Orders@Xlibris.com
38240

Dedication

My grandmother once said that grandchildren are rewards for living well. If that is the case, I have lived well. This book is dedicated to my grandson, Jerry Warren. Jerry has been a pillar of strength for me. He's always there. When the US Army scheduled him for duty beginning the same weekend he had promised to help me move, he informed his Sergeant he would be late. He drove a truck to Vancouver and flew out the next day to fulfill his obligation to Uncle Sam. Thank you again, Jerry. I love you. Grams

Chapter One

In the spring of 1980 I moved to the small town of Payson, Arizona. There were about 5,000 residents in Payson at that time. The living was sufficient as there were retail stores covering basic needs though not much else. I had been recently widowed and after the insurance was settled and the will read, I decided to move to our vacation home in Payson to get away from our well meaning neighbors and family.

My dearly beloved and his best friend went off on their dirt bikes one afternoon. Only the friend returned. As they rode across the California desert, my husband and his bike were literally swallowed by a narrow, but very deep, chasm carved through the desert. The authorities that notified me said they felt the chasm was possibly the result of an earthquake at some much earlier time. It took two days, a large crane and numerous types of earth moving equipment before my husband and his motorcycle were brought to the surface.

The publicity was horrendous. I've never been so tsk'd tsk'd over in my life. I couldn't go anywhere without someone telling me other horror stories about cyclists they knew and their awful fates at the hand of Mother Nature.

And so I went to Payson. I found a job working for a title company doing secretarial work. It wasn't exactly the type work I was used to doing but I was capable enough to do it well. The job was interesting and I met many people who lived and worked in Payson I would not have met otherwise. My job was to type the legal papers that would later be signed by buyers and sellers of Payson properties.

Early one afternoon a man, dressed quite well for Payson, came in with a Quit Claim Deed that needed to be filed and recorded. One of the escrow officers talked with him and I heard her say, "Why didn't you just file this yourself while you were at the County Court?" I wondered how she knew he'd been to the County Court. Later I learned it was the way he was dressed. He normally did not wear a business suit around town.

He wanted the deed recorded soon and he wasn't going back to the County Court anytime in the near future. The deed hadn't been signed when he had gone down earlier that day. The two of them chatted for a few minutes and the escrow officer handed the paper to me and asked that I get it into the filing packet for the afternoon courier. I took it into my office to verify that it was ready for recording before I processed it. It was a Quit Claim Deed from Joseph Ellison to Fletcher Ellison, his brother, for a section of land just north of the Town of Payson. All the i s were dotted and the t s crossed. It had been notarized by a notary with the same address as Mr. Ellison's. I learned later that was his office address and the notary was his long time secretary. The document appeared to be properly signed and notarized so I prepared the request for recording.

I went back to the escrow officer's desk. "Does Mr. Ellison have an account with us or is he leaving a check for the filing?" They both laughed.

Mr. Ellison took out his wallet and counted out the proper fee. The wallet reminded me of a trucker's wallet. Big, overfull, a wallet with a large chain that anchored it to his belt loop. Somehow it just didn't fit the clothes he was wearing. "You got a live one here, Annie. Better keep an eye on her or I'll steal her away. You know Mary Ellen is getting married in a couple of months and I'm not sure she's sticking around Payson."

The escrow officer just smiled. "I think Eleanor knows her job here is safe." I had a feeling Mr. Ellison wasn't worried if I was concerned with my job security. He left the office whistling and jingling the chain on his wallet.

That was my introduction to Fletcher Ellison.

That evening, after work, my coworkers decided to go across the highway to a local lounge and have a drink. This was a fairly common Friday occurrence. As usual, they asked me to come along. I haven't gone with them before but I have just begun to realize that I'll never meet regular towns people if I didn't get out more. So, I tagged along.

The Chalet is a small motel with a restaurant and lounge. The restaurant and lounge are in the front building—I think it's also the registration desk for the motel. The building looks like a Swiss A-frame hence its name, I presume. The general area is called the Swiss Village but other than a line of strip mall across from the Chalet, where our office is, nothing has that Swiss look. I am going to check someday to see if there are, or were, other "Swiss" references around the area.

Duane, our office manager, found a large corner booth that would handle the five of us. It was an hour into the "happy hour" at the bar and the place was filling up rapidly. Duane knew what everyone drank—except me.

"Eleanor, what are you drinking?"

I paused for only a second. "How about an IW Harper and water—tall?"

Duane looked startled. "Wow, I'd never have taken you for a bourbon drinker, Eleanor."

We always drank bourbon when my husband was alive. "Isn't it a ladylike drink?" I asked him. I wasn't sure if there are ladylike and unladylike drinks.

"Oh, I'm sure it is. I've just never known a lady who drank bourbon."

I made some comment that I could drink something else, if he thought it would be better. That struck him as funny and he headed for the bar, laughing. Another of my co-workers went to check out what was on the happy hour buffet table and returned with plates of goodies. Behind him followed a cocktail waitress with a stack of small plates and some napkins. She said. "I see Duane is playing waitress again. I'd better go help him before he drops all your drinks." She took off and got to the bar just as Duane was ready to pick up the tray. There seemed to be some good-natured kidding between them and he took a drink off the tray and sipped at it while following the waitress to the table.

We were nibbling on chicken wings and egg rolls and some small bar-b-qued something or other when Fletcher Ellison came to the table. He was still dressed in a business suit. Duane hadn't seen him earlier that afternoon and said, "Good god, Fletch, have you been down to the County Seat again?" He moved over in the booth so Fletcher could sit down with us.

Three hours and two drinks later, I decided it was definitely time for me to head home. Anne, an escrow officer, had already left saying she had to get dinner started. Fletcher had been telling jokes, some quite bad, and stories of his various conquests for at least two hours. I was actually getting bored. I like a good joke or two and maybe three. But a couple hours worth along with a couple bourbons—well, it was just a tad much for me.

When I slid out of the booth, Fletcher made some comment about going to the little girls' room. I said, "No, actually I am going home."

"Have I said something to offend you, Ellie?" He was suddenly quite serious and almost appeared sober.

"Eleanor. And no, you haven't offended me. It's time for me to go home."

Fletcher eased out of the booth also. "Well, at least let me walk you to your car. You are parked across the street at the title office, aren't you? You should never cross the highway alone this late at night." He poured concern on as thick as honey on warm toast. The sun was simmering on the horizon. It wasn't dark yet . . . maybe 8 o'clock.

"Thank you, Mr. Ellison, but I am sure I can cross the highway safely." I just wanted to get out of there. I had eaten some of the snacks but was hungry. I can't afford to eat dinner at the Chalet as it is one of the pricier restaurants in town.

Fletcher persisted and told Duane to stick around; he'd be right back. He walked me across the highway to my car. I thanked him for his courtesy and got in. "Hey, wait a minute. I thought maybe we could talk for a bit."

"Duane and the rest are waiting for you, Mr. Ellison. I don't want you to keep my boss waiting." I turned the key and the engine fired with a low healthy rumble.

"Wow! That sounds really great. Who's your mechanic?" He tried to lean into the car.

"Oh," I said. "My husband has always cared for this car." I put the car in reverse and started to ease out of the parking space.

Fletcher had that slack jaw look people sometimes get when they hear something they didn't expect. I thought he couldn't be much of a trial attorney—his face is too readable.

"I thought you were a widow lady." He put his hands on the door of the car. "Aren't you?" I could practically see the wheels turning—he had wasted some good time on someone unavailable.

"Yes, I am. But you asked who my mechanic was and George always cared for the car. My kid brother monitors it now." I kept easing the car out of the parking space. He finally stood erect and released his hold on the door.

"Well, okay. I'll see you around." He turned and ran back across the highway. I took the back road home.

And those were my first experiences with Fletcher Ellison, attorney at law. He believes he is a suave, debonair, handsome and witty man. As an attorney he has 'authority'. (He thinks.) He goes through life telling wild and, often, humorous stories. Frequently they aren't funny at all but that doesn't keep him from laughing, loudly, at the end of each of them. He works very hard to impress and that makes me wonder why. He doesn't meet any of my criteria for a successful attorney. Quite frankly, he gives me the creeps. But Mr. Ellison thinks he is wonderful and that is what counts.

Chapter Two

I had been at the title office nearly a month when Duane suggested I take the Arizona Notary exam. He explained that people frequently came in for notary work that was not associated with a deed or title, or anything else we do normally. And, since he and Anne were the only notaries, he'd like to have someone who would be in the office on a more regular basis than either of them.

The exam sounded hard and I hoped I wouldn't have to go to the County Seat to take it. The County Seat, believe it or not, is 96 miles southeast of Payson. As it turned out I could take the exam in Payson and by the end of the next week, I had taken and passed the exam.

My house in Payson sits on a ridge overlooking old town and the south entrance to the town. There are 8 or nine other houses lining Summit Ridge. One afternoon when I came home from work I noticed a sign in the yard of the house next door . . . a foreclosure sale sign.

The Frohms were nice people; and had been good neighbors when I first moved in. But over the past month or so they seemed to be having trouble between themselves. And finally, one Saturday afternoon, one of her brothers drove up with a large truck and helped her move out of the house. From what I could see from my side deck, she took most of the furniture.

The house was quiet and dark most of the next few weeks. I saw Mr. Frohm come and go occasionally but that was about it. One evening as I took a walk I found a large pile of beer cans in the alley below the Frohm house. From the location and structure of the pile I would guess he sat on his back deck, drank a beer and tossed the can below to the alley. I came by the next morning, Saturday, and picked up the cans.

Gus, at the recycling center, asked when I had taken to drinking beer. Or had he missed a party at my house? I told him my neighbor was tossing the cans down to the alley and I didn't like the way it looked. "Besides that," I said. "I can always use the recycling rebate." He said I was very funny as he handed me $2.10.

On my way back to my house I stopped at the post office to buy stamps. As I was leaving, Fletcher Ellison stopped me in the lobby.

"Have you been deliberately avoiding me?" He put his arm across my path. I had to stop or run into him.

"Of course not. Why would you think that?" I was puzzled.

"Well, you haven't been to the Chalet with your office buddies for a couple of weeks."

I screwed my face into a twist and said, "I've only gone with them once."

Fletcher lowered his arm. "And here I thought you were avoiding me."

I shook my head and moved to go around him. The arm went up again. "Why don't you join them next week?"

I was beginning to get annoyed. "Mr. Ellison, I am not much of a drinker and don't really enjoy sitting in a smoke filled lounge with a group of people I've worked with all week."

"Does Duane know how you feel?" He leaned closer to me. I took a step back.

"We've never discussed it. Socializing isn't part of my employment contract. Friday night drinks don't seem to be a big deal to Duane."

He leaned a little closer and spoke just above a whisper. "My dear, you know that can't be so. Duane crosses the highway nearly every night for a drink. Fridays he brings friends."

That did it! "I am not his friend. I am an employee. And I am not a big fan of drinking for drinking's sake."

"Well, maybe you could be a fan of drinking for a good time." He turned slightly toward me and I didn't like it. He was just too close. Fletcher Ellison may think he's suave and debonair but really he's just a short man who isn't even particularly handsome. He doesn't dress well—the first time I saw him was an aberration. Usually he dresses in overalls and flannel work shirts. I think his personality is more than a bit abrasive and this encounter certainly bears that out. I have made no untoward moves on him and his attention is unwanted.

I turned abruptly and headed for the front door of the post office. Evidently he isn't turned down too often. He was quite surprised. "Wait, Ellie." He ran to get ahead of me to block the door.

"Mr. Ellison, my name is Eleanor. I don't like to be called Ellie." Just then Lyle, the town mortician, came into the post office and I took advantage of the open door and left. Lyle, a very pleasant man, saw Fletcher and immediately greeted him. I got into my car and went home.

When I got home, I put the car in the garage. It's probably only the third time I've done that since I moved here. I spent the rest of the day refinishing the side deck. It isn't covered as is the back deck and was showing some weathering. I had hosed it down thoroughly before leaving earlier and now it was dry and ready for new varnish. I am surprised at how long it took. It was past lunchtime when I finally cleaned my brushes.

Feeling absolutely gritty, I took a shower before having something to eat. Just as I got out of the shower, the doorbell rang. I grabbed a terry robe and went to the door. It was a florist delivery person.

"Are you Eleanor Hutchins?" I admitted I was. "Sign here please." I signed and he handed me a long gold box with a broad white ribbon around it.

"Is there a card in here somewhere?" I called after the delivery kid as he climbed my front steps to the street.

"Oh, yes ma'am. It's inside." He got into his truck and drove away leaving me bewildered in my bathrobe.

Coming back inside, I pulled the ribbon on the bow and opened the box. There were white roses nestled in green waxy paper. A card was on top of the roses. "Reconsider and come up to the Chalet for a drink tonight. It's not Friday and I'm not your boss. Fletcher."

I found a vase and arranged the roses. Strange, there were only eleven. I called the florist and he assured me that was the order from Mr. Ellison. Then he added, "He always starts with eleven roses." I started to ask what he meant and decided I didn't want to know.

After I had prepared my lunch, I locked the front of the house and sat on the back deck to eat. I watched the traffic come in and go out of Payson. My elevated viewpoint allows me to see the small mountain pass that was officially the southern city limit of Payson. It's almost two miles from my house to that point of the highway. I spent most of the afternoon on the deck.

I did not go to the Chalet.

Chapter Three

Over the weekend I decided that I would talk to Duane on Monday about Ellison. The man unnerves me. He was parked across the highway from my church on Sunday morning. I attend early service and was rather surprised to see his truck parked on the side of the road. I tried to look as though I hadn't seen him and parked as close to the church door as I could. I didn't look toward the highway as I entered the sanctuary.

On the way home, I came across Main Street instead of the back way as I usually do. On the south side of Main there is a Protestant church. The marquee proclaims "Fletcher Ellison, Pastor". I wanted to be sure that I hadn't dreamed that sign at some time. The church has only one service each Sunday morning that starts just before my early service lets out. Fletcher's truck was sitting in the first parking space of the church lot. Why would he be at my church so early? What is he up to?

Monday morning Anne called the office saying she'd be late. Usually there are just the three of us until Cyndi comes in at 11am on Mondays. I considered this a sign that I should speak to Duane. He didn't appear to be too busy when I rapped on his doorjamb. "Duane, I need to talk to you." He looked up and waved toward the chair in front of his desk.

"What's up?" He laid his pen down and gave me his full attention.

"What's with Fletcher Ellison? He stopped me in the post office Saturday and accused me of avoiding him. Later in the day he sent me flowers and asked me to meet him at the Chalet. I told him I wasn't much of a drinker and didn't care to go for drinks with you all every Friday. Is he always obnoxious like this?"

Duane ran his hands through his hair. "Fletcher thinks he's God's gift to women. Not just single women, all women. He probably hasn't been rebuffed in quite a while."

"Isn't he married?" That was what I heard in the strip mall rumor mill.

"Oh, sure, but he doesn't let that slow him down." Duane pushed himself away from his desk. "He's harmless. But you're probably smart to steer clear of him. He is definitely an alcoholic."

"Duane, that doesn't make sense. He's a pastor."

"Oh, that. Fletcher loves to hear himself talk and is sure he knows everything. He came to town about 20 years ago fresh out of seminary. He picked out the richest available woman in the congregation and went for it. She's more than twenty-five years older than he. She put him through law school when he explained that pastoring wouldn't pay enough to take care of a wife. The year he graduated from law school he married her. After graduation she put up the money for him to open a law office in town. But she also insists that he continue preaching." Duane was standing by the time he finished.

I looked at him in amazement. "You are kidding, aren't you? He actually graduated from seminary? You'd never believe it to listen to his stories. Doesn't his wife get upset with the hours he keeps?"

"Fletcher has her buffaloed. She honestly thinks he has to spend a lot of time outside the office, after hours. After all he is a realtor and an attorney. She's a teetotaler and may not even realize how much he drinks or even that he drinks. His current secretary never knew he drank until she saw him stone cold sober one day." Duane came around to my side of his desk and perched on the edge. "Truthfully, Eleanor, he's not a very nice man."

I got up and thanked him for his openness. "He sends a lot of work our way, Eleanor. That's the primary reason I tolerate him. And he picks up a lot of tabs."

I left his office shaking my head. I hadn't realized how sheltered a life I have lived. I've never met or dealt with someone like Fletcher Ellison. And I believe I could not tolerate him just because he is quick at picking up the tab.

The rest of the week was routine. On Friday Duane came into my office and asked if I would mind making the afternoon deposit on my way home. "That way you won't be here when we migrate across the highway at 5." I thanked him for his consideration and agreed to make the deposit. I went out to Anne, who was finishing putting the deposit together, and told her that Duane had asked me to take it to the bank.

"Oh, good," she said. "I wanted to leave a few minutes early and the deposit was going to slow me down. I'll bring it into you when it's ready." I know that she thought Duane was doing this for her benefit. Little did she know.

The weekend passed uneventfully. I saw a couple walk around the Frohm house on Saturday afternoon. They looked about my age; Arizona plates so they were probably from the valley looking for a vacation home. The summer heat was just turning on in the Phoenix area. Anne and Duane told me a couple weeks ago that we would have a surge of title work at the beginning of summer. People who aren't used to Arizona summers head for the mountains. And, if they find a place for sale, they usually buy. If they come up regularly they'll keep the house for years. Otherwise, they eventually think that the 75 or 80-mile mountainous drive on a two-lane road is too much for a weekend and they put the house back on the market.

My house was like that—bought and sold 4 times in seven years. The Frohm house was also bought and sold numerous times in the past decade.

On Monday morning, the couple I had seen at the neighbor's house was waiting at the door when I arrived to open the office. They had called the realty office on Saturday. The realtor met them at the house and showed them the interior and all the stuff that realtors do when they show a house. Then the realtor called and left a message for Duane. Anne checked messages before the end of day Saturday and called him back. The clients were at the Chalet for the weekend. They wanted to buy the house. Less than ten minutes after I opened the office, the local realtor came in with Anne right on his heels. The realtor was Fletcher Ellison.

Good grief! Does he have a finger in every pie in town? Duane had told me that Ellison was a realtor but it must have gone went over my head. Is his law practice so slow he has to dabble in other things? Maybe so, according to the telephone book there are seven attorneys in this little town.

I put on the coffee while the four of them met in Anne's office. When it was brewed, I transferred the coffee to a thermos carafe. I fixed a tray with cups, saucers, spoons—all the usual trappings of a coffee service and took it into Anne's office. I set the tray on the credenza behind her desk and left as unobtrusively as I could. The door had not been completely closed so I left it ajar when I went out. I saw Fletcher go to the coffee tray and he poured a cup of coffee. As we used to say when we were kids, he played mother and offered coffee to everyone. Such a show!! You got the impression that he was the host and you were in his office, not the title office up the street.

I went back to the kitchen and made another pot of coffee.

In about an hour the meeting in Anne's office broke up. The Bayhs are buying the house out of foreclosure and will be up at the end of next week to sign the final papers. Everything should be finalized by then. Anne contacted the bank for foreclosure figures during the meeting. Mrs. Bayh wrote a check for the foreclosure satisfaction. Anne will take that to the bank later and get a release signed. Fletcher offered them another tour of the house that morning. Mrs. Bayh wanted to check for electrical outlets and such.

The three of them left around 10:30 and I went in to collect the coffee tray. Anne said, "I really appreciate that you do this. Everyone is so much more at ease with a cup of coffee." I was trying to remember how the custom had started and couldn't. Someone must have asked me to serve coffee when I first came. Oh well, it makes no difference. Anne was happy. And I don't mind making coffee.

It was my day to have lunch at noon. We trade off lunch times so everyone would have a chance for a couple 'uncrowded' lunch days. If we have a doctor's appointment or something we always knew which day we have a late lunch that can stretch a bit into the afternoon. It is a convenient arrangement.

I frequently go home for lunch but didn't feel like it today. I walked to the restaurant at the far south end of the strip mall where our office is located.

There is a hostess but she was busy. I scoped out the seating. To my horror, Fletcher and the Bayhs were sitting in a corner booth. It was too late to walk out now. Fletcher saw me and he excused himself to the Bayhs and walked to where I was standing.

"Aha! Got cha. You can't refuse to have lunch with us. It would look bad to our mutual clients. We just got here so come sit down."

I was totally ticked but he was right. I didn't want to look like a jackass. Too bad there wasn't someone else I knew that I couldn't have latched on to. Putting on my most gracious smile, I followed Fletcher to the booth.

As it was a booth, and the Bayhs were sitting next to each other, I ended up sitting next to Fletcher. He patted my knee at least twice. I shot him a nasty look both times and he just smiled. Other than that, it was a pleasant meal. The Bayhs had many things in common with my late husband and me. There were times we actually forgot Fletcher was there. John Bayh is a mechanic; Carrie an accountant/secretary. They have no children at home. This is to be their vacation home though they think they'll both look for work here and move up permanently as soon as it is practical.

Fletcher asked Carrie if she had ever worked for an attorney and she said that she had for two years. She found it to be boring as it was primarily real estate law. He gave her the pitch that his secretary was getting married this summer and perhaps Carrie would be interested in working for him if Mary Ellen moved out of the area. Mrs. Bayh said she'd certainly consider it.

Our food came and I ate more quickly than usual. I explained that I had the early lunch today and didn't want to keep the next person waiting. I asked the waitress for my check and she told me that Fletcher was picking up the tab. I was surprised. I could understand his picking up the Bayh's lunch—he was in for a 6% commission. But mine? He said, "Please, Ellie. Don't argue."

"Eleanor, Mr. Ellison, Eleanor." I wasn't going to let him get away with it just because there were strangers present. "Thank you very much for lunch." I addressed myself to the Bayhs. "I'll see you when you come in to sign the final papers. If you have any questions regarding the closing, don't hesitate to call Anne." Mr. Bayh stood up as I excused myself and offered me his hand.

"See you a week from Friday." He shook my hand. I sort of waved at both of them and left the restaurant. It was then I realized that Fletcher's office was right next door. It was a logical choice for him to take clients there. I was a bit put out with myself for not thinking he'd invite them to lunch. And, that he'd choose this restaurant. Some days my brain doesn't go into first gear and I miss the obvious.

I hurried back to the office. That man really bugs me. Letting him pay for my lunch bugs me even more. Grumble, grumble.

Chapter Four

This afternoon the paper has a help wanted ad for the naturopathic clinic on Aero Drive. This sounds like something Carrie Bayh would be interested in and I folded the paper into their escrow folder. I am anxious for them to move to Payson. I think they could be good friends as well as neighbors. The more I thought about it, the more I worried about someone else calling on the ad before the Bayhs returned. I looked through their escrow file and found Carrie's home number. I called and left a message on her answering machine that there was an ad in the paper she might want to call on before she got here at the end of the week. I read the ad to her machine including the contact information. I told her to call me at home if there were questions and I left my number while reminding her that I was the secretary at the title company. I wasn't sure she'd remember me.

I should have known better. Carrie Bayh is such a people person that she called me around 6pm and said, "Did you actually think I wouldn't remember you?"

I said, "Well, I just didn't want to take any chances. Let me tell you what I know about the doctor who owns and runs the Aero Clinic." She said she really appreciated this and asked if I thought she should wait until tomorrow to call. I suggested she call as soon as we hang up and leave a message. I was pretty sure the doctor checked messages if they weren't actually rerouted to his home.

About forty-five minutes later, Carrie Bayh called back. She has an interview at the Aero Clinic the afternoon they come up to sign the final papers. She and John were both going to take off at noon that Friday. They'll be at the title office as soon as she interviews. She is almost as jazzed as I am at the possibilities. I had already said goodbye when she added, "Eleanor, call us Carrie and Jack. Mr. and Mrs. Bayh is just too formal."

It's a great summer evening in Payson. I made my dinner and took it out on the back deck. I love watching the traffic in and out of town. I doubt that

19

the traffic will be this heavy during the winter. There aren't any fireflies in Central Arizona but watching the flickering headlights and taillights is just as entertaining. I have a small ice cream parlor type table and two chairs on the deck—bright yellow and just right for one or two people. I also have a glider swing and spend a lot of time on the deck.

Around 9:30 we are in almost total darkness, so I think it was that late when I saw a large vehicle coming up the hill below my house. There was a rack of running lights across the top of the cab. Suddenly I realized that it was Fletcher's truck. I dashed into the house and locked the front door and made sure there were no lights on. Damn, the car is in the driveway. I stayed in the shadows on the deck and watched the truck labor around the last curve of the paved road. Then I heard it shift down and knew it was on Summit Ridge. I slipped inside the house and locked the back door. Where could I go in the house that I couldn't be seen from any window? Maybe my bedroom—but the garage is an add-on and if someone came into the garage, they could look into my bedroom windows. So I went to the master bath. Those windows are frosted though accessible from the back deck. I made sure those windows and the bedroom windows were locked. I left the bathroom door open to the bedroom and pulled the telephone into the bathroom.

I realize this sounds really, really radical. But have you ever gotten the creeps after meeting someone? If so, you know what I mean. I don't like talking with Fletcher one on one anywhere. And I certainly don't want him in my home.

I heard the large pickup pull into the driveway behind my car. There was no slam of the door. Maybe he didn't shut it. There were footfalls on the gravel driveway and gravel path around the garage and then on the steps to the back deck. I saw a shadow cross the bathroom window. I heard a rattle of the back doorknob. I heard the footsteps cross over the side deck and come back around to the front of the house. Then the front door was tried. I could hear the footfalls on the front gravel pathway. Wait. Now it sounds like someone is in the garage! I could hear someone fumbling around in the dark. Then a metallic thud. What the heck could that be? The bedroom windows rattled. Thank god I had locked them. Someone is standing on the washing machine! The washer and drier sit under the bedroom windows. Unbelievably, someone is standing on my washer! After another few minutes I heard footfalls on the driveway again. There was a long, long pause. Nothing happened. No sound of a person—or a truck.

Finally, nearly half an hour after I had seen the truck come up the road, it roared to life and I heard the door slam. I hoped he had control of the truck—the driveway is steep and I am afraid he'll roll into my car. There was a wild revving sound and gravel flying. At last I could tell he was back on Summit Ridge and then turned back onto the main road. I opened the bathroom window and watched the truck roar down the hill.

It's a good thing I did. He didn't head for home; he didn't leave Old Town. He pulled into the parking lot of the Winchester Saloon at the bottom of the road. I went back out on the deck without turning on a light. I stayed there until the saloon closed and he finally drove across Main Street and out of town. I believe he was waiting for me to either turn on a light thinking he was gone or to come home and turn on a light not knowing he'd been there.

The next morning I went into the garage. There were footprints on my washer and dryer. I called the police. The officer wanted to take a detailed report and I asked if the report would be public record. Why? I told him I was sure I knew who the party was but he was an attorney and I didn't want him to know I knew he'd been at my home.

The officer looked at me with a surprised look on his face. "Are you saying Fletcher Ellison is stalking you?"

I hadn't mentioned any names so now I was the one with the surprised look on my face. "I didn't say stalking. I merely said that a person went around my house, rattling all the door knobs and climbing on my appliances to gain access to my bedroom windows."

"Fletcher Ellison." The officer said his name again.

"I didn't say that." What part of privacy doesn't this officer understand?

"Mrs. Hutchins, the department is aware that Fletcher Ellison has sent you his famous bouquet of eleven roses. We have a deal with the florist. Ellison doesn't like to be rebuffed. Usually the situation works itself out but he has never climbed on a washing machine before. You have evidently refused to succumb to his obvious charms." The officer was being facetious and I resented it.

"Yes, I am sure it was Fletcher Ellison. At least, it was his truck. But I don't want him to know I was at home. Is there some way to write the report so he won't know?"

The officer said there was; and he would. And then he asked, "Are you aware all the tires on your vehicle are flat?"

"What?" I ran out to the driveway. There sat my little car with four flat tires. "What am I going to do now? This had to have happened last night."

The officer went to his radio said about three words. Then he asked if he could use my telephone and spoke to someone for quite a time. When he came back he said that Fred Friendly would be up in an hour or so and repair the tires. "How much do you suppose that will cost?" I have a job but I'm not rich.

"Friendly Tires is on contract with the PD. We'll handle the cost. It'll be a part of the report." The officer got into his cruiser and took off—straight up Summit Ridge. I was more shaken than I thought and found myself sitting on the steps outside the garage. My knees weren't working too well. I sat there about half an hour and finally pulled myself up and went into the house.

Did Fletcher think I wouldn't know who did this? Or that I wouldn't find out? If he was interested in establishing a relationship with me, he was showing it in a most peculiar manner. How could I ever feel safe around him after this? I don't even want to speak to him again. I hope he doesn't come into the office anytime soon. Being civil toward him is going to be difficult. I'm not a very tactful person as it is.

I had barely quit shaking when a truck with several utility boxes attached pulled into the driveway next to my car. I had never met Fred Friendly though I have passed his yard several times. I greeted him as warmly as I could muster.

"Wow! We may have to replace this one. The air was let out of the other three tires but this one is punctured." He pointed to the left back tire. I couldn't see how he could tell the difference. How could he tell the air was let out of three and not the fourth. I didn't see any holes; just flat tires. Then I saw the valve caps sitting on the hood of the car. Three valve caps.

"I've only had these tires since March. How much will one new tire cost?" My dad had always told me to try and keep four matching tires on the car. I paid a lot of money for four and could only guess at the price for one. And, would he have a match?

Mr. Friendly had gone to work on the three flat tires with a small generator and a long air hose. "I am sure you want a matching tire. Fortunately, this style is still available—we can match the others. As to cost, Chief Rose says to send him the bill. Don't worry about it."

"How can you get paid that way?" I had never heard of the police taking care of vandalism.

"The PD has a 'victim's fund' for people like you who have been monetarily injured through absolutely no fault of their own. About every six months they hit Ellison, and other high profile citizens, up for a donation to the victim's fund. I don't know why in hell they won't just throw his ass in jail. It was Ellison that did this, wasn't it?"

I told him that I really didn't know but the officer thought so from the footprints and the dual tire prints. Fletcher Ellison has the only dual wheeled pickup in town.

Mr. Friendly just shook his head and went back to work. He came onto the back deck to tell me he was taking the slashed tire back to his yard to be sure he matched it exactly. Michelin has two very similar tread patterns. I offered him a glass of lemonade and he accepted. He sat down on the glider swing with me and rocked back and forth gently.

"Mrs. Hutchins, steer clear of that man. Well, evidently you have or you wouldn't have this problem." He finished his lemonade and said he'd be back in half an hour or so. He had just backed out onto Summit Ridge when I saw Fletcher's large pickup coming up the paved road. I ran out to the street and waved at Mr. Friendly.

"He's coming up the hill. I don't know if he's coming here but he's coming up the hill." I was trembling. I didn't realize how frightened I was of Fletcher Ellison until that very moment.

Mr. Friendly pulled his truck to the side of the Ridge, blocking my driveway in the process. He got out of the truck and stood there next to me. "Just be cool. He doesn't have to know we know he's coming."

The rack of running lights on the cab appeared over the top of the hill on Summit Ridge. Then the entire truck was visible. He seemed surprised that the driveway was blocked. He reached over and rolled down the passenger window. "Hey, Fred, move your truck. I've come to rescue the lady."

"The hell you say. Rescue her from what?" Mr. Friendly is a very large man. He stands a foot taller than Ellison and outweighs him by a hundred pounds.

Fletcher flinched noticeably. "Well, I heard on the police radio that she had a flat tire."

Quietly, I said to Mr. Friendly, "The officer used my phone, not his radio, to report the tires."

Fred said, "You must be mistaken, Fletcher, the lady called me on the telephone. She needs a new tire is all." And that was exactly how it looked— three tires full of air and the fourth wheel on a jack stand.

Fletcher didn't look too happy and slammed the truck into gear. The tires spun before they took hold and he left at an unsafe speed for the little mountain lane. Fred ran to his truck and picked up his microphone. "Hazel, call the PD. Ellison is flying off Summit Ridge eastward and should hit Wade Lane doing at least 60 miles an hour."

I think the police car must have been in the area as less than a minute later we heard a siren. Mr. Friendly said, "Now I'll be back in half an hour."

About this time I am rethinking living a peaceful life in Payson. I can hardly wait until the Bayhs move in next door. Will that help? Probably. If not, I guess I can always move back to Mesa. But after the clean air, the trees and the hummingbirds—I don't think I can be happy in Mesa again.

The police officer had photographed the footprints on my washer and dryer and so I cleaned them. I didn't clean the windows because I wasn't sure if the officer had taken fingerprints. This man left fingerprints all over my house for Pete's sake. He had to have done so—he knocked and rapped nearly every window and door. Do eleven roses and lunch give him a right to harass me? I don't think so. It appears the police know he's dangerous. Why *don't* they lock him up?

Mr. Friendly had just replaced the punctured tire when the florist truck arrived. The same delivery boy came down the driveway to where I stood and handed me another long gold box with white ribbon bow. I said, "Please wait a moment." I was sure he would as I hadn't signed for the delivery yet.

Mr. Friendly was wiping his hands on a mechanic's rag when I opened the box on the hood of my car. White roses. I pushed the waxy green florist paper aside and counted. I took the card and retied the bow around the box. I handed it back to the delivery boy. "I'm sorry. But I cannot accept the flowers." The kid's mouth dropped open. I suppose no one has ever refused white roses before—or any florist delivery for that matter. He got back into his truck, with the box, and left. He was shaking his head in disbelief. I guess.

Mr. Friendly asked, "What was that all about, Mrs. H?"

"They were from Fletcher Ellison. The first, and last, bouquet was made up of eleven roses. I called the florist and he said that was Mr. Ellison's standard order. But there's only ten in this box. I wonder what that means?"

"You could call the florist and see what he says. Maybe Ellison has some sort of pattern." Mr. Friendly put his tools away. "I'm laying odds he does."

"Do you want to wait and find out?" I headed for the back door and the telephone.

"Sure," he replied, "why not? Damn sick bastard." He came up on the deck and poured himself some more lemonade. "Hey, what does the card say?" I had forgotten I had it in my hand.

I read the card aloud. "Ellie—I came on my white steed to rescue you. You should have allowed me the privilege. Fletcher"

"That man is sick. Do you suppose he slashed your tire just so he could show up and be a hero?" Mr. Friendly stood shaking his head. "I'll bet he parked somewhere and listened to the police radio dispatch. Then, knowing the officer wouldn't do anything but take a report, gave it an hour and he showed up."

"I don't know. You could be right. I am going to call the florist." I went into the house to the phone. I dropped the card in a bowl by the door—with the first card.

I came out shaking my head. "You're right. It's a pattern. Each bouquet Ellison sends has one less flower than the one before it. When he gets down to one he told the florist he'd come in, pick it up and deliver it himself. I had to ask. So far he's never gotten to one."

Mr. Friendly left the deck and got into his truck. He started to back out of the driveway and then stopped and stuck his head out the window. "Girl, if you have anymore trouble with that sicko, call me. Hazel and I are in the phone book. We live behind the shop—that's a mile down the road. If you need help, call. I'm sure Hazel won't mind. She thinks Fletcher Ellison is a psycho anyhow. This little story is going to convince her of that." He backed out of the driveway, waving as he dropped below the crest of the hill.

I pulled the car into the garage and locked the garage before going back into the house.

The rest of the week slipped by. I called Duane to let him know that I was on my way to work and I'd explain when I got there. I went the back way hoping I wouldn't run into Fletcher. I was sure he was still on the loose; with a speeding ticket in hand, but on the loose. I was sure of that based on what I'd heard from the investigating officer earlier. He'd be ticketed if seen; so the prowl around my house couldn't put him in jail. No one saw him—not even me. Even with his boot prints and fingerprints, for some reason that man would not have to pay for his misdeeds. Why? But, he would get a ticket for speeding because he was actually seen by a police officer. I wonder if he could get someone in the judicial system to fix the ticket?

And ten white roses . . . what the hell do they mean? What was the florist trying to tell me? That every woman Ellison chases eventually allows herself to be caught?

Chapter Five

On Monday morning Carrie Bayh called me. She had called the Aero Clinic again for more information on the job and talked with the Dr. Richards. She had the job—sight unseen. He still wanted to talk to her but he'd hold the job until they were both satisfied Friday. She was quite pleased and had just given her notice at her current job. She was that positive about Dr. Richards. She said, "We'll be up Friday to sign the papers. Can you have dinner with us?"

I said that I could and would be delighted—especially since they would be my neighbors. We were both excited when we hung up.

I was so glad that this was a foreclosure sale. The bank prefers to close escrow immediately. The Bayh's excellent credit and connection with their own bank had provided immediate credit to complete the sale. All they had to do was sign the final paperwork. It would be filed and recorded on Monday as the courier for Friday recordings would already be gone by the time the Bayhs got to Payson.

There were two walk-in notary requests this week. Anne was out of the office and Duane asked me to handle them. The first entries in my notary log—wow! Duane says I can keep the notary fee if I want. I thought since he paid for the exam and bond that he would want any fees.

By the time Friday lunchtime arrived I had promised myself I'd eat lunch "out". I wondered where I could go and get back in an hour. The restaurant next to Ellison's office was definitely off limits. Anne suggested I go down the highway to Pedro Wong's. She said, "They're almost fast food. And there are a couple of picnic tables in the back under a ramada. You can eat there, go home or come back here."

I took my purse, got in the car and off I went. The menu was a delightful assortment of Chinese and Mexican food. I'll have to ask Anne how the name came about. My number was called in about 5 minutes and I went up to claim my lunch. Just as I turned around Fletcher Ellison came in the front door. I wasn't sure he'd seen me and I left by the side door less than ten feet from where I was standing.

My car was sitting right outside that door. I hadn't realized there was a door there when I drove in as it's not marked. I was backing out of the lot when Fletcher came out the front door waving his arms. I pretended to not see him and turned left on the street that intersected the highway instead of pulling on to the highway. I don't know why I did that. This little lane intersects with another major street that turns north and comes out behind the KFC. I waited impatiently at the traffic light and returned to the office as soon as possible.

Thinking about my return route, I realized that little street also intersects Wade Lane and I could have gone home from there. But, as I had seen Ellison, I sure didn't want to go home. I began to wonder if he came in for lunch; though Pedro Wong's doesn't seem to be his speed. Or had he seen my car in the lot?

Anne told me that the owner of Pedro Wong's had a Chinese father and a Hispanic mother so he thought using his own name would be appropriate to sell food of the two cultures. I told her I didn't care what he called the place. The food was incredibly delicious. No fast food taste—really good food. She laughed at me. "You're one of the few people I have ever known that gets excited over food."

I guess I do.

Around 3:45 Jack and Carrie Bayh came in to sign the final papers and turn over the final money. I believe I have never known a couple that seems so full of life. They obviously care for one another very much. Neither of them are large people—Jack maybe 5 feet 8 and Carrie about 5 feet 2. He has black hair and snapping brown eyes while she is blonde and blue eyed. They appear to be a perfect pair. I am enthused that they'll be moved in about two weeks. Now that Carrie has a job here, Jack is going to commute part-time and stay with Carrie's folk a day or two a week until he had work in Payson.

"That means that a moving van and I will be pulling into our new house two weeks from tomorrow." Carrie was quite enthused and she lit up the entire corner of the La Casa Piquena lounge. She had seen the restaurant on their way to the title office and thought it would be a good place for dinner. We had arrived at 5:15 and Jack decided we should have a drink in the lounge first. He left his name with the host and asked that we be seated in an hour.

The owner came over to the table to speak to me and I introduced her to Jack and Carrie as "my new neighbors". She was most gracious and bought the first round. "Thank you so much, Sandi. By the way, Carrie is going to work for Dr. Richards at the Aero Clinic."

Sandy said she was delighted. The doctor's wife had been doing front and back office duty for the last six months and it was beginning to take a toll on her good nature. We all laughed. "Come on, admit it. The Doc is one of the most gentle and nicest men in town." She agreed and said she had better get back to work.

That hour was the quickest hour passing I have experienced in Payson. Carrie told Jack and I all about her interview with Dr. and Mrs. Richards. She said that she felt as though she had known them forever. We discussed the neighborhood and the town. We went into dinner around 6:30. They are going to stay the night and return to Chandler in the morning.

Jack is concerned about landscaping their new house. Like mine, their house is built on a narrow ridge. The back yard falls 50 feet to an alley. They were both worried about erosion and wondered what they could plant on that slope to keep it from running away. I said that George and I had put in a retaining wall at the bottom and planted about 40 azalea bushes on our backyard. They said they'd have to go back and look at both yards in the morning. "Come to think of it, there isn't a retaining wall at our place." Jack mulled that over for a moment and then said, "Can you recommend a mason to build the wall?"

I was just ready to respond when someone behind me said, "Of course I can. That's part of the service." Oh, no, it was Fletcher Ellison.

Jack stood up and greeted Fletcher. I swear he is the most polite man I've ever met—Jack not Fletcher. And Fletcher thinks it too. "Mind if I join you? Have you ordered yet?" Jack admitted we hadn't even bothered to look at the menus yet—we were too busy landscaping the back yard.

"Well, Ellie here knows all about that. She's got the best looking backyard on Summit Ridge." He smiled at me thinking he'd get away with the Ellie remark. He evidently thinks I am polite too. Ha. He doesn't know me at all.

"Mr. Ellison, for once and all, could you please call me Eleanor or Mrs. Hutchins? No Ellie, please." He looked at me as if to say he thought I'd not say anything.

"Bad memories or something with the nickname?" Why did he want to pursue this?

"No, not at all. I've never been called Ellie, never. And, at my age, there's no need for a nickname now." He looked slightly deflated. But it didn't keep him from sitting down with us. He called the waitress over and asked for the usual; double olives. In a few minutes she returned with a martini.

He made a ceremony out of the first sip. He closed his eyes and appeared to take a deep breath. He exhaled slowly and said, "Perfect. Gin—it's the only way to make a true martini." He and Jack discussed the merits of various drinks and Carrie and I looked at the menu.

When we had finally ordered, Fletcher looked across the table at me and said, "You were very bad when you refused my roses. I don't appreciate being made to look the fool."

"No one knows but you, I and the florist. Well, now you've told Jack and Carrie." I didn't flinch as I'm sure he expected. "So, unless you've told someone else, only five of us in the whole world know that I an unappreciative."

Jack and Carrie sat there with puzzled looks. Fletcher picked up his martini, removed the two olives and downed the remaining drink in one gulp. Before he sat the glass on the table he had his hand in the air for the waitress. When she came to the table, he merely pointed at the empty glass. She turned and headed toward the lounge. He munched on the olives.

When a new martini was in front of him, he turned to Jack and said, "I've been trying to getting on Ellie-nor's good side ever since I met her. And all she's done is rebuff me." He went through the ceremony of first sip without comment.

Jack picked up the drink he had brought with him from the lounge and pretended great interest in it. I think he was a bit surprised at Ellison's demeanor. I know I was.

"Back to this mason who's a part of the service." Jack was trying to get the conversation back to a cordial level.

Fletcher pulled a pen out of his overalls and lifted a napkin from beneath his martini. "You can call John in the morning and I'm sure he'll meet you at the house. You can discuss what you need and he should have it finished by the time you move in."

I could tell Jack is the type of guy who likes three estimates for everything. Living in a town where there isn't three of everything was going to be a new experience for him. I said, "John is very professional. He built my retaining wall. He's quick and not over priced." Fletcher beamed at me as if I had just pinned a medal on him.

"It's nice to know that we agree on something, Ellie-nor." He seemed to be waiting for a correction but I wouldn't give him the satisfaction. It's close enough for me.

I continued. "And as for azaleas, if that's what you decide for the slope, there's a man in Star Valley who grows the sturdiest plants I've ever seen. I can get his number for you tomorrow."

"Not to worry, little lady, Ray is a friend of mine. And I just happen to know his number." He added 7 digits to the napkin and wrote flowers after them.

Evidently there is only one azalea grower in Star Valley, a blip in the road east of Payson. I had found Ray's Gardens by accident.

Dinner was served just then and the conversation gradually returned to its original friendly, non-competitive attitude. In the next hour, Fletcher had redeemed himself, at least outwardly, with the Bayhs. He was charming, witty and picked up the check. Jack protested but Fletcher insisted it was 'part of the service'.

He went into the lounge as we left the building. Jack and Carrie both wanted to know what was the thing about the roses. I told them, trying to keep it low key. Jack turned to Carrie and said, "Well, Sweetie. I guess you are right about Fletcher Ellison."

It was my turn to ask, "What, what?"

Jack said that on their way home two weeks ago Carrie had proclaimed Fletcher Ellison to be a real nut case.

Chapter Six

The following Monday the masonry truck pulled into the alley below the Bayh house. I was watering my back yard (translate that as slope). John saw me and walked to a spot below me. I turned off the nozzle.

"How are you, Mrs. Hutchins?"

"Just fine, John. How have you been?"

"Things are going well. Thanks for the referral on this retaining wall. Mr. Bayh said you gave me a great recommendation." He began pulling tools out of the truck.

"Come on, John. Is there anyone else in Payson that lays block like you do?"

He admitted there probably wasn't. "But I still appreciate the vote of confidence. This is a good job, you know." I nodded. I knew. It wasn't that long ago that he built my retaining wall. For Payson it may have been expensive;but in Mesa it would be quite inexpensive.

By the end of the week, the wall was completed. Like mine, in addition to the cinder block there was a façade of wooden beams. The wall looked like mine—very, very elegant, yet rustic.

A week after the wall was done, a large moving van pulled into the driveway next door. Right behind the van was Carrie and Jack, in separate cars. It was about 11am. I went over to see if I could be of some help. Jack said he thought it was under control but he'd appreciate it if I could stay on call—one never knows. The first thing he did was walk down the slope to look at the retaining wall. "That is one good looking wall, Eleanor. Thanks for the recommendation." I almost said something about Fletcher Ellison but evidently Jack feels the recommendation had been mine. He ran back up the slope and around the house to the moving van.

Carrie was directing the unloading—where this goes, where that goes and Jack was helping unload. I went home and made several sandwiches and put them on a tray that I covered with a dishtowel. I had made a couple salads last night. I filled a large thermos jug with lemonade and another with iced tea. I saw a small table placed on the Bayh's back deck just about then so I carried the thermos jugs over. I returned home for glasses and one of the salads. It took about four trips to get everything to the Bayh's back deck.

I went around to the front and told Carrie that lunch was on the back deck whenever they needed a break. She looked at her watch. "My gosh, I didn't realize it was so late. The van was loaded yesterday but we left Chandler at 8:30. Hey, guys, lunch is ready." She directed placement of the furniture they had out of the truck and then led the way to the back deck. "Thanks so much, Eleanor. I was thinking of running down to KFC or something. This is a lot better."

I said, "And, you'll save a lot of time as well." She grinned about that and watched the guys wash up at the kitchen sink before they went out on the deck, drying their hands on their jeans.

Jack was standing there with a plate full of salads and a sandwich in his hand. "Eleanor, thanks so much. This is great. I was starving." He finished the sandwich in four or five bites and reached for another. One of the moving men went to the van and pulled out kitchen chairs. Soon we were all enjoying a quick lunch. I left the thermos jugs and glasses, cleaned up the rest and returned home.

The van was empty in another two hours. Everything was in its place. Of course, part of everything was in packing boxes. There would be a lot of work to do after the van was gone. I was in my front yard watering when they all gathered at the back of the truck. From my vantage point I saw Jack tip the movers. They shook hands and by 4pm the van was gone. Jack picked Carrie up and twirled her around. He let out a whoop that carried all the way up the Ridge. They went into the house.

Isn't it wonderful? I have neighbors my age—right next door. I didn't want to intrude so continued watering. I figure they'll let me know when I'm welcome. I can remember the excitement George and I shared when we moved here. Payson has an air about it . . . clean air. You get kind of heady up here in the mountains. I put the hose away; washed my hands and picked up the one half remaining sandwich before going to the glider on my back deck. What a pleasant evening it was turning out to be.

About 7pm I heard footsteps on the path leading around the garage. I got up just as Carrie came up the deck stairs. "Our telephone isn't installed yet. I hope you don't mind my intrusion." She had changed clothes and looked quite relaxed. She had my thermos jugs in her hands.

"No problem. You didn't have to bring those back tonight." I took the jugs from her and set them inside the kitchen door on the counter.

"Oh, this is a social call. Jack's taking a shower and sent me over to ask if you'd care to go to dinner with us. And to ask where we could probably eat without running into Fletcher."

I had to admit that I wasn't too familiar with his haunts. "But, in all the time I've lived here, I don't remember ever seeing his truck at the Oxbow." I pointed out a stone and wood building next to the saloon at the bottom of the hill. "I hear it's an older place that cooks a good steak. But, I've never been there so can't swear to it."

"If you haven't seen him there, I think we should take the chance. Jack will be dressed and ready in about 15 minutes. Is that too quick for you?"

I looked how neat and crisp she looked and said, "It'll take me maybe ten minutes. Shall I walk over when ready?" She thought that would be a great idea and I walked her back up my driveway. Then I dashed into the house to wash up and change into something a little less casual.

We lucked out. Fletcher never showed. I wanted to ask someone if he ever came in but was afraid it'd jinx us. We had a great dinner and a lot of conversation. Much of it dwelled on the back yard. I told them that Ray's was open on Sunday. If they wanted to go out tomorrow and see what was available they could. We made a date to meet at their house at noon the next day.

It was after 10 when I got home.

I am feeling good about Payson again.

Chapter Seven

On Monday afternoon Ray delivered the plants Jack and Carried had selected Sunday. On Tuesday Carrie and I planted 25 azalea plants on their back slope. "How come you seem to have more room than we do back here?" Carrie asked when we had stopped for iced tea after the first ten plants.

"My house sits across three city lots; yours on only two. Of course, half of my third lot is straight downhill there at the west end of the property." She got up from her deck and looked across at my house.

"So, you own that little point of land just as the hill drops?"

"Yep, funny how they consider that a city lot—there's less than 20 feet of flat ground." We chuckled over city politics and properties and went back to work.

They had also bought a peach tree and an apple tree to be planted in the front of the house—one on either side of the sidewalk. I have a peach and apple tree in my front yard and Jack thought they looked downright snazzy. We decided we'd leave the trees for Jack to plant. They were in five-gallon cans and are a bit unwieldy. Carrie wanted to get some unpacking done before she starts her new job next week. She'll be working Monday, Tuesday, Wednesday mornings and Friday. We both think that is an odd schedule—having Wednesday afternoon and all day Thursday off. But the pay is good for Payson.

We worked at unpacking and putting things away Wednesday. Mainly, I unpacked and she put. We had a good rhythm running and were making great progress when her front door bell rang. It was the telephone man. They discussed where she wanted jacks and type of service, etc. I looked at my watch and interrupted to say I was going home to make dinner. She should come over or call when she was finished.

"Here is Payson we have only one prefix, 474. So when you ask someone for their telephone number they'll probably only give you four digits. Mine is 1695."

Carrie laughed and said, "There are so many differences already. I hope it doesn't take me too long to adjust to small town living."

The telephone installer put in his two cents—"In a month you'll wonder how you ever managed to live in the valley. I guarantee it." I agreed.

My answering machine was blinking when I came in. Twenty-two messages! What? If I get two a week, it's unusual. I got out a pad and pencil to take down the information. I'd never remember twenty-two. There was no voice on any of the calls. Some heavy breathing, nothing said. On all twenty-two. I called the police department and asked them if there was anything I could do about this. They asked if I had any idea who might have done it. No, I didn't. They said there really wasn't much they could do then.

I started dinner without erasing the messages. I wanted Carrie to not hear them. I made a salad and set the table on the deck for dinner for two. Jack had gone back 'down the hill' to Carrie's folks in Mesa but would be back on Wednesday evening. I have a small ceramic grill—sort of a hibachi—that my Dad gave us when we bought this house. I moved the end table from the glider closer to the table and set the grill on it. The chicken breasts I had taken from the freezer and put in the fridge that morning were thoroughly defrosted. I put them into a marinade while I finished making the rest of the meal. In about 20 minutes, Carrie yoohooed from the garage steps. I appreciate that she gives me warning she's on premises.

"I was going to call but figured you're only next door."

The coals were perfect and I transferred the chicken from the marinade to the grill. "Wow! Eleanor, that smells great. What's in the marinade?" Carrie was on the glider sipping a glass of wine.

"It's one of my dad's recipes. Has ginger and honey in it." I poured myself a glass of the chardonnay and turned the chicken over.

"Ask your dad if you can share the recipe. I think Jack would love it. He says if something smells good, you're sure to love it."

I put a piece of chicken on each of the dinner plates. "Would you like a little more wine?" She nodded and handed me her glass. I pulled the wine bottle out of the ice bucket and refilled both glasses before sitting down.

The meal was as good as it smelled and we ate a lot. And we talked, a lot. We really like each other and I can foresee a long friendship between us. After we finished, we cleared the table and loaded the dishwasher. Then we decided to go back to unpacking. I locked everything up. Carrie looked me and asked, "How come you're locking everything up? Jack and I thought Payson was safe to leave stuff open."

I put the keys in my pocket before answering. "It is safe. But someone has been giving me a bad time and I just don't want to come home to a house that may have someone hiding in it."

"Fletcher?" She looked at me in a sideways look. "It's something to do with the roses and stuff, doesn't it?"

I just nodded. I really didn't want to go into it. Then I remembered the answering machine. Unlocking the door, I said, "Wait up a minute. I almost forgot. I want you to listen to something." She came back into the house with me.

Turning on the dining room light, I hit the play button on the answering machine. After about the 10th call, Carrie asked, "How many calls are there?"

"Twenty-two."

"Twenty-two? Good lord, who is it?"

I turned the machine off. "I don't know. The police say there's nothing they can do."

She just shook her head. "This is ridiculous. Absolutely insane."

I turned out the light. I locked the door again. We went next door and back to work. We worked until about 11. I came home tired, took a shower and fell into bed. The telephone started ringing about midnight.

After two calls with no response to my hellos, I turned the bell off on the bedroom phone and went back to bed. Let the answering machine handle it.

The next evening I went to Carrie's and left my front porch light on. It can be seen from Summit Ridge but not from any of the streets below the house in Old Town. When I came home, the answering machine was filled again with empty calls. Carrie and I had a short list of suspects. Actually, a list of one. But we had a non-existent list of reasons.

From that day on I began to leave at least one light on in the house that could be seen from Main Street below. Carrie and I have decided that the calls are from someone watching the house. If I'm home, no calls. If it appears I am not home, a lot of calls. And, when that happened, the calls would begin again as soon as I went to bed and turned the lights out again.

Fletcher doesn't live in town. And he's never been known to frequent the Oxbow or the Winchester—the two places with a bar visible from my back deck. So, even my short list wasn't very reliable.

Leaving a light on when I was out of the house in the evening seemed to calm things down. I still locked every window and door when I went out and kept things pretty well locked when I was home. This was not the carefree living I had envisioned just a year ago.

Chapter Eight

In the next week or so I didn't see Fletcher Ellison around town. That doesn't mean he wasn't there. I was just fortunate enough not to run into him. I had gotten back to my pre-Fletcher carefree way of living. Down to the market, the post office, bookstore, whatever, whenever I wanted to go. It was a great feeling. I stopped in at Friendly's Tire Service and met Hazel. She's a real nut . . . I mean that in a good way. She and Fred are a perfect pair. They play off each other a lot as George and I used to do.

She was full of town news and knew just about everything that was going on. I took an immediate liking to her.

Then one late afternoon, on a Wednesday, Fletcher Ellison came into the title office. "Hey, Duane, what are you doing this afternoon? I need a notary." Duane told him he had two couples coming in to sign closing papers and Anne was on vacation.

"Sorry, Fletch, can't help you today." Duane sat back down in his chair.

"Duane, please, I have a whole family of wills in Gisela that need to be witnessed and notarized. They were supposed to come in last week and the old lady got sick. Mary Ellen's on her honeymoon this week. I need a notary." Fletcher whines pretty good. I half smiled to myself in the safety of my little office.

Duane came to my office door—which was open. "Eleanor, Mr. Ellison needs a notary to go with him to Gisela this afternoon. Would you please go?"

I think I paled visibly as he said, "Are you all right?"

I nodded. "I'm fine but I would rather not go anywhere with him, Duane. Please, don't ask me."

Duane turned around and called out to Fletcher. "What time would you be back in town, Fletcher?"

Fletcher came to my office door and stood next to Duane. "There are five wills. They say there will be plenty of witnesses. They own the Bar-b-q

Pit in Gisela. There are always people there. Maybe 2 hours. If we leave now, we'd be back by 6."

Duane turned back to me. "We can bill Fletcher up the whazoo, Eleanor." This was an in-house joke. Billing, I was always harping on billing. "Come on. It's a chance to get out of the office."

I did not want to go. I was afraid to go. I am afraid of Fletcher Ellison. I know that Duane knows about the tire episode. Why would he do this to me?

"Eleanor?" He wanted me to do this.

"Okay, let me get my stuff." I was trembling as I got out my notary ledger, seal and embosser from the desk drawer. I put them into my briefcase along with half a dozen pens. No one ever has a pen when they want something notarized. I picked up my suit jacket, my purse and my briefcase and stepped out from behind my desk. Under my breath I told Duane, "I do not like this. But I'll do it because you've told me to do it."

I followed Ellison out to his truck. I am not sure of the make or model but it is a huge pick up truck. There's a rifle rack in the back of the cab—but no rifle. There's a rack of running lights across the top of the cab. And, the rear wheels are dual wheels. There is a little step like thing on the passenger side of the cab. I opened the door and put my stuff inside and heaved myself up into the cab using the little step. Heave is the only word I can think of—it was an effort to get into the truck. I am just over five feet tall and I think that the step is three feet in the air. Even long legs aren't helpful. And there was no good handhold. Damn.

Fletcher didn't offer to help me. He was behind the wheel waiting for me. "A little short in the leg, huh, Eleanor?"

"No, sir, I have long legs. It's just a longer step up." I folded my jacket across my lap and sat back.

He turned the key and the truck growled. Off we took. Gisela is a very small town south of Payson a few miles off the main highway. It's maybe 20 miles. Once we left the main highway, the road was unpaved and quite bumpy. I was thoroughly shaken by the time we got to where we were to meet his clients.

He pulled up in front of the restaurant and slammed on his brakes. I guess, to make a show, he came around to my side of the truck and opened the door and offered me a hand down. After letting me crawl in by myself, this was a surprise. But welcomed. I reached back into the truck and got my purse and briefcase. I left my jacket in the truck. Fletcher was in overalls. I felt over dressed as it was. The title office requires business suits or neat skirts and tops. I wear dress shoes but not high heels as the other women in the office usually wear. I'm just not into really high heels.

There was a lot of glad-handing as we walked in. The entire family was there. Fletcher pulled out five blue backed documents and a file that appeared to be copies from his briefcase. He introduced me as his notary. It took half an hour to get everyone lined up to sign his will. And, each person had a couple friends there to witness him signing his will. Arizona is a self proving will state so wills are both witnessed and notarized. Unless the notary knows the signers each person has to produce identification as well.

But first, we had to accept something to drink. I asked for root beer or club soda. The bartender actually snorted. I leaned toward him and said, "I am supposed to be very sober when I notarize something. If someone thinks I wasn't they could contest the will."

"Oh, yeah, right." He said. Then he turned around and asked me, "How about Fletch. Doesn't he have to be sober too?"

"No, he had to be sober while he was putting the will on paper. But his job is done now." I thought to myself that this was the stupidest position I've ever found myself in. It's nearly 5 pm and we are just now ready to sign the first will.

Actually, once the process began, it went fairly smoothly. But still, it was after 6 by the time everyone had signed their will and my ledger and the witnesses had all signed everything and I had notarized all the wills and completed my notary ledger with identifications, etc.

Then the family insisted we stay and have dinner on the house. The aroma in the restaurant had increased significantly over the last hour and it made me hungry. Without asking, Fletcher accepted for both of us and we were led to a table by the front window.

Fletcher was drinking some imported beer. The bottle has a white-hinged cap that snaps snuggly to a rubber gasket around the bottle's mouth. I think he likes the bottle more than the beer. There was so much preservative in the beer I could smell it across the table. He had quite a few and I was getting a bit leery about the return trip to Payson. Once we get on the highway, it's almost straight up hill for eleven miles. It's a treacherous mountain road in the daytime, when you're sober. I dreaded thinking what it'd be like in the twilight with a drunk behind the wheel.

Dinner was superb. I complimented the chef and found that the old man of the family had created the sauce. It is an incredible taste. He told me I could buy a pint of it if I wanted. Two bucks. I thought that would be great. He gave it to me in a brown paper bag and I wedged it into my briefcase. Even with a gasketed lid on the jar, I didn't want to take any chance of ending up with sauce all over my ledger and briefcase.

It was nearly 8 when Fletcher decided he was ready to leave. He just got up and looked at me, "Are you coming?" Of course, I was. We're 20 miles from home. I gathered up my stuff, left a tip on the table and scrambled into the truck. No help in. Either he was not interested in making an impression upon leaving or he forgot I was along. He started the truck before I had the door closed.

We bumped, bumped, bumped down the dirt road to the highway. He geared down and put his foot in it. I realize it's a large truck and it's a steep grade, but I thought he might be overdoing it.

Twilight is very fleeting in the mountains. Tonight was no exception. By the time we had careened through the first two major curves on the highway north, it was dark. Fletcher turned on the lights and trod more firmly on the accelerator. When we were almost at the top of the long grade, he sort of waved toward my side of the road.

"I live right out there about two miles." I saw a little signboard but we were going too fast for me to read what it said.

Speed increased and increased and we were doing over 80 miles an hour by the time we reached the crest of the hill by the Reservation. "Mr. Ellison, could we slow down a bit? We're almost in town."

It was as though I had awakened him. "What?"

"Can we slow down a bit?"

"You don't like the way I drive?"

"I think we're going a little fast—we're almost in town."

The truck slid slightly to one side as he slammed on the brakes. "Well, I don't live in town anyhow. I was just doing you a favor by taking you home. But, if you don't like the way I drive, you can get out here." The truck shivered as it came to a complete stop.

"Go on. Get the hell out of my truck." He was yelling as loudly as if he was trying to get my attention from a block away. "Get out!"

I could see the back deck light on my house. I could see the light on the Bayh's back deck. I am only two miles from home. I gathered my purse, jacket and briefcase and slid out of the truck. Luckily, I landed on my feet. I was worried about my pint of bar-b-q sauce but couldn't smell anything so figured it was still whole. Before I could turn around and close the door, he slammed the truck into gear, made a u-turn across the median to the opposite side of the highway and left me standing by the side of the road. I heard the door slam as the truck righted itself on the highway.

Many hours of sitting on my deck had prepared me for this. Of course, I didn't know it until now. There is a small street almost directly across the highway from where I was standing that T's into the highway. It goes straight north and T's into Main Street directly below my house. I carefully crossed the highway and walked the 50 or so feet to find the beginning of Mclean. It was so dark. No moon to light my way. Eventually my night vision kicked it and I could make out the edges of the little street.

I am sure glad I don't wear high heels. I stumbled up the road for a few feet and said to myself that I'd have to be damned careful not to break an ankle. I can't tell from my back deck what condition this little road is in. It's not that great, actually.

Then I remembered a small penlight my Dad had given me a few weeks ago. I had dropped it into my purse. I felt around the bottom of the purse and found the penlight. It was small but bright. In less than half an hour I was at Main Street and followed Mclean up the hill to Summit Ridge. The incline to Summit is quite steep and it took more energy to climb the last 50 yards then the entire walk had taken. I entered my house by the front door.

Instinct had been to turn on all the lights. Or turn off the back deck light, or both. Then I decided that I would try to keep the house dark. I have no clue if Ellison was going home or not. He was quite drunk and he might decide it's too early to go home. He might also decide to give me a bad time. I locked up again.

In the bedroom, I pulled the drapes. In the bathroom, I put a heavy towel over the bathroom curtains. I want to take a shower but don't want anyone to see a light. Yes, I am paranoid. This man scares the bejebbers out of me. There is no sense in taking chances.

Just as I stepped into the shower I remembered that my car was sitting at the title office. He was supposed to return me there. Well, I can walk to work in the morning . . . it's just over a mile. But I begin to fume again. Wait until I get hold of Duane tomorrow.

I was out of the shower and getting ready for bed when I heard footsteps in the gravel by the garage steps to the deck. I turned off the bathroom light. The footsteps went the length of my back deck and across the side deck. I could just imagine someone peering into the dining room and living room windows. But I wasn't moving any further than the bedroom. Then I heard a noise I know I know. But, I can't place it.

Suddenly a flash—whomever is on the deck is now sitting on my glider swing. That noise is the squeak of the chain as the glider moves back and forth. I picked up the bedroom phone and, by feel, dialed the police. When they answered I whispered, "This is Eleanor Hutchins on Summit Ridge. Someone has just come up on my deck and is sitting on my glider. Could someone check it out? But don't come up Mclean—the street is visible from the deck."

The officer asked if I knew who it was. I said, "No. I was getting ready for bed. I believe that whoever it is doesn't know I'm home. I left my car at work today."

There was nowhere I could really go in the house, other than the hallway, without taking the chance of being seen. And then I could go only as far as the front bath. I would be visible anywhere else in the house from one window or another. I just sat on the edge of my bed and waited. About two minutes later I heard footsteps both in front of the house and by the garage. I hadn't heard a vehicle but there were now two more persons on my decks.

Suddenly there was a scuffle. "What the hell? Let go of me! Who the hell are you?" The person on the glider was Fletcher Ellison!

"Payson PD, Mr. Ellison. A neighbor called saying they thought they saw someone enter Mrs. Hutchin's deck and they believe she is not at home."

"What damn neighbor? What business is it of his?"

"Come on Fletcher. On your feet. Where's your truck? How did you get up here?" There was more scuffle but not as violent.

"Good god, Ellison. You're drunk as a skunk. What are you doing up here?" I could only hear mumbling. The police covered my call and didn't knock on the door. "We're going to have to call Mrs. Hutchins to see if you're an invited guest."

"She's not home. I tried to call her." Fletcher was yelling.

They wrestled him off the deck and into the back of their patrol car. I don't know how they managed to get to my house without my hearing their engine. They must have coasted down the Ridge from the opposite direction.

After I heard the car drive away, I went into the dining room to the answering machine. It was blinking. There were 14 calls—no words, just empty calls. I guess he tried to call me all right. Was he actually worried about my safety? Whether or not I got home? Or is he worried I am going to complain to Duane? He must have called while I was walking home. I was to ticked to look at the phone when I came in.

Thinking Fletcher was in custody, I slept pretty well that night. Whether or not he was in jail is another thing altogether.

The next morning, just as I was ready to leave the house, the telephone rang. It was Duane. "You naughty girl. Your car is still at the office."

"Naughty my ass. I have to walk to work because I did what you told me to do yesterday. I had to walk over two miles to get home last night because Ellison was drunk and I asked him to slow down. He made me get out of the truck by the Reservation. Then later he shows up at my house even drunker and I called the police. I don't know if he's in jail or if they turned him loose. But, don't you ever ask me to go someplace with Fletcher Ellison again." I slammed the phone down into its cradle.

The phone rang. It was Duane, again. "Stay right there. I'll come get you and you can tell me the whole story in a calmer tone. Okay?"

I said, "I have told you the whole story but you can get me to work. I am pissed; at you and at Ellison."

He was there in five minutes. I relented and told him the whole story of the day before from getting into the truck at the office to getting out of it on Highway 87 in the dark of night.

"And on top of everything . . . this was a part of the will service. I don't get paid."

Duane said, "Yes you will—we'll bill Fletcher up the whazoo."

And we did.

On Friday, 9 roses were delivered to the office. The card blew my temper back into a fury. "You should not have allowed me to drink so much. Fletcher" Duane and Anne thought it was funny. I was livid. What a jackass this man is.

I felt I had to justify my reaction to him to Duane and Anne. "He was doing 90 by the time we got to the Reservation entrance. You know the speed limit is 35 from there into town. I sure as hell didn't want to be pulled over by the PD. I don't want anyone to know I ever was in that truck with that drunk."

Duane and Anne thought I was being a bit melodramatic. But Duane said he'd not ask me to do something like that again. He did apologize. I didn't take much comfort in the apology.

Chapter Nine

The summer passed pretty quickly. By Thanksgiving Jack had a job in Payson. He and Carrie included me in a lot of their doings. We have neighbors across the street—much older than all of us but charming people. Charles and Mary. Charles had been a bartender before retiring. An invitation to dinner at their house included at least one drink before dinner, an appropriate wine with dinner and fantastic after dinner drinks. It was a good thing we live so close. If I had to do more than cross the road, I'd never make it home.

The five of us formed a dinner party circuit. Sometimes it was just the five of us; sometimes we'd invite someone who didn't live on Summit Ridge and sometimes we'd invite other neighbors on the Ridge. We always have a grand evening. Charles was a marvelous chef and he cooked up some great dinners. Carrie was a good cook and she'd counter his great dinner with her marvelous cuisine. Then I had to cook above both of them. It was a lot of fun. And, a lot of work.

The telephone calls after I've gone to bed were infrequent but persisted. I was going to unplug the telephone in the bedroom but worried that if I did, someone might actually try to call me who I want to talk to and I wouldn't hear the phone. It is a Catch-22 that I will have to learn to live with. I am not happy about it but there doesn't seem to be many options.

Jack had been in Payson fulltime about a month before Carrie got the news that Dr. Richards was closing the clinic. He has been diagnosed with prostate cancer. He has a friend in Mexico who says he can cure him but it requires daily treatment. So, Dr. Richards was leaving Payson and moving to San Marcos. Carrie was devastated.

Of course, as she puts it, their expenses are greatly reduced now that Jack is in Payson. And, they could make it on one salary if they have to. Dr. Richards gave her a month's notice and we all started looking for work for her.

Shortly before the clinic was scheduled to close, Fletcher Ellison came in to collect some records for a personal injury case he was handling. While waiting for Carrie to finish photocopying the file, he asked, "Do you have anything lined up yet?" He was very casual in his asking.

Carrie admitted, "Not yet."

Fletcher told her, "Payson is a pretty dead place in the winter. It might take you a couple months to find work."

She acknowledged she was aware of that but wasn't panicked. As she put all the copies into a file folder, Fletcher touched her on the shoulder. "Mary Ellen has decided that she and her new hubby want to live in Prescott. I am looking for a secretary. Let me know if you're interested. It's not all real estate law so I am sure you wouldn't be bored. The position is full-time, five days a week but I pay very well."

Carrie handed him the file. "How much is well, Mr. Ellison?"

He quoted a figure that almost made her whistle in surprise. It was definitely above the going rate for Payson.

"Let me talk to Jack and get back to you." At that moment Carrie wanted to turn him down immediately but thought she'd talk to Jack first.

"Hey, great, fine. I'll look forward to hearing from you. Mary Ellen wants to leave at the end of the year." He took his file and left. Carrie sat down hard. What a spot to be in. She doesn't like the guy. And, could whatever type of law he practices really be less boring than the last time she worked for an attorney? Maybe the fruitcake boss would make up for a lack of interesting cases.

Carrie could hardly wait to get home and talk to Jack and me. "Geez, what next?" Payson was quite a town. She wants to keep working but jobs are scarce. "Am I desperate enough to work for Fletcher?" She didn't know. She needed some feedback from us.

That same weekend I was going to the valley to do some shopping with my Mom. I don't like the idea of her working for Fletcher but told Carrie, "You know what he's like outside the office. He definitely drinks too much. Maybe he's actually a good attorney. He might be entirely different inside the office. It's up to you. You could take it and then if he seems too squirrelly, you could leave. What does Jack think?"

"He pretty much agrees with you. And that the reason you are having trouble with him is just because you aren't attracted to him as he obviously is to you." Carrie wasn't convinced but thought her husband and I were probably both right. "Oh, Eleanor, while you're at your Mom's do you suppose you might be going into town and to a good department store? I would like to get some more of this cologne but no one in Payson carries it." She went to her bedroom and brought back a glass-fluted bottle with a gold crown cap. There was a very low level of green liquid.

"This is my fragrance too. I am definitely buying some when Mom and I go to Goldwater's. Do you want one bottle or two?" I took out my list and added "Emeraude for Carrie".

"Two would be great. Let me get my purse." Carrie started back into the bedroom with the bottle.

"Don't worry. I am not sure how much it is. You can pay me when I get back. It's about $18 a bottle—or so, I think."

Carrie stopped in the hall. "If that's all, definitely two bottles? If you can, that is."

I said something to the effect that two bottles would be no problem. Then added, "I had better get going. My parents expect me for dinner."

Carrie gave me a hug and walked me back to my house. I had already put my suitcase in the trunk. Being wary of leaving things on that should be off, I went into the house to be sure everything was off and the house locked. On impulse, I turned on the back deck light. Maybe the answering machine won't be so jammed with calls when I get back Sunday.

I was past the turnoff to Roosevelt Lake when I got the brilliant idea that maybe my Dad could give me some advise on using a timer for one of the lamps in the family room. That room faces the back deck, so a lamp on would show. I'll do just about anything to get the answering machine free of empty calls. Then I got the incredible idea that maybe I should just disconnect the answering machine. Why hadn't I thought of that before? I guess sometimes you can get too close to a problem to properly see it. I am going to disconnect the answering machine as soon as I get home. And put a lamp on a timer.

It's been more than a month since I've been to my parents' home in East Mesa. We have had one day of snow already in Payson. They are still sweltering in 90degree heat. Dad says it's been a most unusual year for weather.

The next morning Mom and I drove into downtown Mesa as soon as the breakfast dishes were washed and put away. She had a small list of things she wanted to get for Christmas. My mother shops in July for Christmas. I couldn't believe she had anything left to buy. Well, that's my Mom.

We went to Goldwater's first. It is such a lovely department store. Everything seems like crystal and gold—the aisles are wide. And, it smells good too. I couldn't find my list. I did remember that both Carrie and I wanted Emeraude so I bought four bottles first thing. My mother chided me for losing my list. I can't figure where I could have lost it. I had it in my hand when I went back to the house to lock up. I don't remember putting it down. But, then, I don't remember putting it in a pocket or purse either.

There weren't that many things on the list and I think I was able to recall them all. After Goldwater's Mom wanted to go to Dillard's and Diamonds. These are all high-end stores and nothing like them in Payson. Like Goldwater's the décor is quite elegant in the other stores.

We had lunch at a little place in Tempe. It was a house built with lots of river rock and wood. Ninth and Ash—odd name but clever as that was also its location. I thought it to be a bit pricey but Mom wanted to eat there. The service was most gracious and probably worth the extra dollars. Lunch was pleasant. We talked about all sorts of things including men. Mom thinks I am too young to be a widow. I keep telling her that George was my best friend as well as my husband. Until I find another best friend, I probably won't remarry. She doesn't really understand that. She and Dad have been married forty-six years.

We stopped at the produce market on Apache Trail and bought some veggies for dinner. Mother had a pot roast slowly cooking all the while we were shopping. I bought some fruit that in Payson would cost a bit more—if it is even available. There are some drawbacks to a small town. The Safeway store looks like every other small Safeway in the state. But I am quite sure they tailor their merchandise to fit the area and a lot of things are never stocked.

Sunday morning Dad, Mom and I went out for breakfast—a routine established years before. We had an hour of conversation. I got caught up with the aunts, uncles and cousins and, of course, my brother. Dad asked how the new neighbors were working out. I told him I couldn't be happier, or luckier. They are really great people.

I decided to leave mid-morning. There are a couple things I really need to do at home before the weekend is gone. I left with promises to come back sooner, than later. Dad said, "You're too close to be away so long."

"Dad, the road is the same distance from either end. Why don't you two come up for Christmas? We might even have snow."

He chuckled about that. "I haven't driven in snow for so many years, we'd have to come by dog sled."

"If you want to come, and there is a chance of snow, I'll come get you. It's just over an hour drive and I don't mind." They both said they'd think about it. When I was a kid, their thinking about it usually ended up a no. I hope that isn't still the case. It would be nice to have someone in the house for Christmas. Heck, I might even buy a tree if they decide to come.

Carrie started her new job today. She came home all excited. Ellison's office is the only attorney's office in town that has a word processor. Mary Ellen gave her basic instructions for it. She tried to explain it to me and ended up saying it's like an electric typewriter with a tv screen. You can correct errors or make changes without retyping the whole thing. It takes two disks to operate. But she said they don't look like disks; they're about 8 inch squares. One disk is a program disk. The other is a work disk. Every client file has a work disk in their file. So whenever you do something for a particular client, you have to use his disk.

When you think the document is ready, you can print it on this printer thing connected to the word processor. Then Fletcher looks it over and if he has corrections or additions, he makes notes on the paper copy and then she can go back to the work disk and make the changes without retyping everything. I kept shaking my head and saying, "I see." "Oh really?" and other stupid replies because I haven't got a clue what she is describing. Maybe some day when Fletcher is out of the office, I'll walk down and see what this machine looks like.

Carrie stopped almost every night this week to tell me more about this word processor. She says the actual work is a piece of cake. And there were templates for major pleadings and the wills and stuff. She also said that Fletcher isn't in the office a whole lot. Guess he's being a realtor part of the time too. He interviews the client and gives Mary Ellen and Carrie the notes. Mary Ellen says that usually there is something in the program disk that pops right out at her.

"But you don't know the programs. How is that going to work?" I was worried that she'd decide the job was simple and screw up. What's wrong with me? She's a grown and intelligent woman.

The next day Carrie stopped by with a printed list. It was a print out of the templates and various programs stored on the program disk. "Wow!" I looked at the list. "I am impressed. This is amazing." Carrie just beamed. She was enjoying this job a lot. Mary Ellen would be around for another week or so and Carrie thought she'd be ready to solo by the time Mary Ellen left.

Chapter Ten

Christmas is getting close and Duane says he wants to take the office staff and their spouses or special friends to dinner this Friday. He and Anne are both married; Cyndi has a boyfriend but Jim and I will probably go alone.

Duane said he was thinking of making reservations at Diamond Point Shadows. Had I ever been there? Oh, yes. When George and I first bought the house we went to Diamond Point Shadows for dinner a couple times. It's primarily a steak house, steaks you can cut with a butter knife.

Cyndi, the receptionist and file person, is all excited. She's never been to Diamond Point Shadows. Duane asked if Darrin, her boyfriend, had but she didn't know. He asked if 6pm was okay with all of us. We can leave work at 4:30. The restaurant is east on the highway a pretty good piece and we'll meet there at 6. Jim lives in one of the trailer parks south of my house off Main Street and asked if I would like him to pick me up. "No sense in both of us driving when we live a mile apart." He's a great guy in the office and he doesn't seem to drink a lot.

I said, "That would be great, Jim. If you don't mind coming up the Ridge." He indicated that wouldn't bother him at all. But could he come a couple minutes early and see if he could see his trailer from my deck?

"Sure that would be fine—what time? 5:30?" I love showing off the view from my deck. 5:30 would give him ten minutes or so to scope out the view. I got the impression that Duane expected us to dress up since we had an hour or so between leaving work and getting to the restaurant. Well, I have a couple days to decide what I can wear that isn't over the top for Payson. I really don't know how people dress when they dress up here. Stupid, huh?

By the time Friday came, I had found an emerald green silk palazzo pant suit in my closet. I had forgotten it. George bought it for me when we were taking dance lessons four or five years ago. The pants are like a long full skirt.

It still fits and I can wear my black pumps with it. I am beginning to get into a party mood. Dinner might be a lot of fun.

Jim arrived a couple minutes before 5:30. He's a kid—about 28, I think. "Gosh, Eleanor. Is that really you? You sure look different with your hair up and all dressed up."

"It's me all right." I was flattered. "Come on out on the deck. You will be surprised how far you can see from here." He followed me out and stopped suddenly.

"Is that the highway into town?" He pointed toward the south limits of town.

"Yep, it is. At night you can see the headlights bob up and down as they crest the hill by the Reservation. And, look here, to the west. There's the municipal golf course."

He was surprised at how far he could see. "Is that Pioneer Cemetery over there?" He pointed northwest on the other side of the golf course.

"Yes, it is." I went back into the house to put another pin in my updo. I don't usually wear my hair up and am not too secure about it staying put. When I finished, I went back out to the deck. "Ready? It's quarter of six."

"Oh gosh, yeah." He scurried back into the house. "I don't want Duane to get mad at me for making us both late."

"Jimmy, don't worry. He'll think I wasn't ready." I locked the house and turned on the deck light and the front light. Jimmy has a nice little red pickup and he opened the door for me. He even checked to be sure my pant legs were inside before he closed the door. And off we went. Jimmy talked about the office a bit and we had a pleasant drive to our Christmas party.

As it turned out there was no traffic. The light snow from the day before had literally disappeared. There were little piles of snow under bushes and trees but the road was as clear as if it had not snowed. Diamond Point Shadows is the only building for miles in any direction. It seems so isolated that I have wondered if the owners thought the towns would gradually grow out to them. Or, perhaps the isolation is part of the attraction? I don't know.

Cyndi and her boyfriend arrived after we did. Duane had asked that we not be seated until everyone was there. He told the owner he thought it might embarrass the last person in. We sat in the bar and enjoyed a drink—Cyndi was about 15 minutes late. She was dressed to the nines and, if you didn't know her well, you wouldn't have recognized her at first glance. She's quite a pretty girl, though like many kids her age, she wears a lot of makeup. Her boyfriend, Darrin, wore a white shirt and tie under his parka.

When we were all seated and had menus, Jimmy leaned over to me and whispered, "This is a pretty nice place. Have you eaten here before?" We had been seated at a large square table in front of the burning fireplace. It is impressive. Open beamed ceilings; wrought iron chandeliers; very nice.

I whispered back, "Yes, my husband and I used to come here occasionally. The New York steak is especially good."

Almost everyone ordered the New York cut . . . except Cyndi and Darrin. They ordered prime rib. Salads came; Duane ordered 2 bottles of a good red wine and everyone chatted casually while waiting for dinner. Suddenly, the front door flew open and a draft of cold air circulated around our table. Tony, the owner, ran to close the door. Just as he got there, Fletcher Ellison came in, stomping his boots as he came.

He spotted Duane and came right over. For a change, Duane didn't invite him to sit. The way the table was arranged, there was no room. He stood and made small talk. Then he went to the bar and got an empty wine glass and returned to our table and poured himself a glass of wine. Cyndi and Jimmy's eyebrows went up in surprise.

He had been at the table a good five minutes when he looked over at me and said, "Ellie-nor. is that actually you? You certainly look charming tonight."

I didn't know what to say. Duane came to my rescue and said, "We are at a company Christmas dinner. Everyone looks exceptionally fine tonight—even me." He laughed at his own joke and we all sort of giggled along.

Fletcher came around the table and stopped directly behind me. "Ellie-nor, you look so fine that I am offering to take you home. I didn't see your horse out front so you must have come with someone."

I couldn't really look at him. He was behind me. "Mr. Ellison, I am not the sort of woman who comes with one man and leaves with another. I'll go home with the person I came with."

He didn't seem to react to that. But, as I couldn't see him, I wasn't sure. I looked to Duane for guidance. I hoped he was reading my "get me out of this" message I was sending him mentally.

He was. "Fletcher, please don't get all crazy on us. Eleanor is part of my staff and I will see that she gets home safely."

"Crazy? Are you insinuating that I am crazy?" Fletcher put a hand on my shoulder. I didn't move. Thank goodness I didn't flinch either.

"Of course not, Fletcher. I just want to treat my staff to a private little dinner party." Duane looked like he wished he could just get up and lead Fletcher out of the restaurant.

Fletcher was leaning in so closely to me now that I could smell beer on his breath. He drinks martinis usually and the last time I saw him drink beer, I ended up walking home.

Fletcher stepped to one side of me. He took his big trucker's wallet out of his back pocket and unzipped it. He leafed through the contents until he came to a folded piece of paper. "I am not crazy and I can prove it." He ceremoniously unfolded the paper and laid it down next to my salad plate. "See? What does that say there at the top, Ellie-nor? Read it out loud for the people."

I blinked at what I saw. Was I really seeing this? "Department of Mental Health, State of Texas."

"Go on, read the rest." He pointed at the second paragraph.

"This is to certify that Fletcher C. Ellison is determined to be of sound mind and is hereby released from the care of the Department of Mental Health, State of Texas." I quit reading aloud. White male, aged 16; I took a quick look at the date on the bottom. 1964. He had been in a mental institution until he was 16? I don't see any other dates but wonder how long he'd been incarcerated!

"How many of you can prove that you are of sound mind?" Fletcher began waving the paper in my face. "How many of you can prove you're not crazy?"

Tony, the owner of Diamond Point Shadows, had started into the dining room with a waiter and our dinner order. He said something to the waiter over his shoulder and set the tray he was carrying on the end of the bar. He walked quite spryly to our table and to where Fletcher stood.

"Fletcher, my dear friend, come into the bar with me. I want you to sample this new gin that I got today." He took Fletcher by the elbow and it appeared he was not going to take no for an answer. Fletcher took his release paper and began refolding it.

"A new gin, Tony? What is it?" Tony had diverted him and took him through the far door into the bar. Meanwhile, another waiter came and picked up the tray Tony had been carrying. The two waiters served our dinner.

I was a bit shaken. I didn't want to ruin the evening and so made some trite comment about the appearance of dinner. Duane looked more shaken than I. Only Duane and I knew of my episode of notary work for Fletcher. Duane picked up his wine glass. "A toast—to good friends and co-workers. Merry Christmas."

We all raised our glasses and said, "Merry Christmas."

The steak was as tender as every other I've eaten at Diamond Point. Jimmy was impressed. At one point he leaned over to me and said, "I actually cut my steak with my table knife. I wonder why they give you a steak knife?"

"I think it's just custom. People expect a steak knife when they order a steak."

He nodded. "That makes sense. But you sure don't need one."

Duane had asked for a special dessert . . . cherries jubilee. I have had this dessert before and so had Anne and her husband. But it really impressed the younger members of our staff. Big eyes as the flames flared up. Duane sort of smiled and whispered something to his wife. She nodded and smiled.

Duane asked Darrin and Jimmy if they thought they could drive home safely if he ordered an after dinner drink for us. We'd been there over 2 hours and Jimmy thought he surely could. He hadn't had more than a beer when we came in and a glass of wine. Darrin said, "Sure."

Duane signaled for a waiter. "We would like eight King Alphonse, please."

Again the kids looked at each other questioningly. We old fogies enjoyed watching them. The drink was served in a proper glass and impressively layered.

About 45 minutes later, we were ready to leave. Duane said, "Well, this is a Christmas dinner so I guess gifts are in order." He gave each employee an envelope containing a greeting card and a check. Anne and I were surprised as neither of us had cut checks for him. "Anne, the list is on your desk so you can post the checks next week." She smiled. He is a thoughtful person.

We began saying goodnight when Duane got up and went toward the bar. He looked in briefly and came back to the table.

I was putting on my coat when he came around the table to Jimmy and me. "Fletcher is still in the bar. Crystal and I will go keep him occupied while you get out of here. Jimmy, head straight home. Okay?"

Jimmy nodded. "But isn't the door out through the bar?"

Duane said, "That's how you came in—there's another door over there." He pointed to the opposite side of the room. "Cyndi, Darrin, don't leave by the bar entrance. Follow Eleanor and Jimmy out, okay? If you want another drink this evening stop at the Moose Lodge and tell them I sent you."

He said he would wait five minutes after we left before he and Crystal would go into the bar. Jimmy said to me, "You'll tell me what this is all about on the way home, won't you?" I promised I would. And I did.

It was snowing ever so lightly as we pulled out of the parking lot and started back into Payson. I tried to fill Jimmy in on my recent run in with Fletcher. He said, "I don't care what that paper he has says. That man is nuts."

I agreed.

It wasn't as late as I had imagined when we got home. I asked Jimmy if he wanted to come sit on the deck and watch it snow. He thought that would be a marvelous idea.

"I really want to be home by 10:30 though." He's into some television program that he didn't want to miss.

"It was just an idea. You aren't obligated. I just thought you might like to see how the town looks with a snow sprinkle."

"Hey, I never did check to see if I could see my place from here." He stepped out on the deck.

"It's kind of dark, Jim. Have your oriented yourself to where your house would be?" I pulled the door shut behind us and turned out the deck light. "Let's see, if you live on Aero—" I pointed almost straight down. "The first street with streetlights is Main. The next street with street lights is Aero."

"I left my porch light on," he said. "It's green so maybe I can spot it." We both looked across Aero and suddenly he said, "There it is. See?" He pointed a bit to the left. Sure enough there was a green porch light. "I can see my place from here. Someday if I need a ride or something, I'll hang a yellow flag out. Okay?" He was laughing as he said it.

"Sure enough, Jim." I pulled my coat closer around me. "I come out on the deck every single morning. If I see a yellow flag down there, I'll call you to see if you need a ride or something." I said it with a very straight face.

He looked at me and said, "You would, wouldn't you?"

"Of course, we're co-workers. And if you ever see a red flag up here you'll come running. Right?" He laughed and nodded.

Jimmy looked at his watch. It has a lighted dial. "I've got to get going. Thanks so much for the evening. I appreciate your explaining things to me."

I wasn't sure what he meant. I didn't remember explaining much of anything to him all evening. Other than about Fletcher. I walked him through the house and let him out the front door. He had parked at the side of the road. As he drove off, I locked the front door and turned off that porch light. Then I went back to the deck and watched his little red truck go down Mclean and turn on Aero. In a minute his porch light went out and his inside house light came on. I wished I could remember what program he told me he was going home to watch. I'm not much into television but thought it'd be a pleasant change to fill the evening.

Overall, it had been a pleasant evening. Duane's wife is delightful and Anne's husband has a very wry sense of humor. He had us laughing through half the meal. Cyndi's boyfriend is a real redneck sort of guy but he seemed to enjoy the meal—especially dessert. He had said, "I've never seen anybody set food on fire on purpose before." That brought a big laugh from the entire table.

Yes, it was an interesting evening.

Chapter Eleven

Jack and Carrie went to the valley to spend the weekend with her folks. The neighborhood was very quiet. The light snowfall of Friday evening was already gone from the roads. Saturday morning the golf course was a beautiful white blanket of snow—but by noon it had all melted away. I ate my breakfast Saturday on the deck, wearing an old heavy sweater to keep the chill at bay.

Eight white roses were delivered late afternoon. Rather than have another run in with Fletcher, I accepted them. The card read "Merry Christmas. Your faithful servant, Fletcher Ellison." Your faithful servant? What planet was he on when he wrote the card? I put the roses in a tall green glass vase and set them on the coffee table in my living room. They were beautiful. I couldn't help but wonder how much roses cost in December.

I brewed a large pot of tea and went out on the deck to watch the world. Late afternoon there were footsteps on the gravel by the garage. Since Jack and Carrie were gone, I couldn't imagine who it might be. Charles, across the street, always called before coming over. He could never tell when I was home if I was on the deck and decided it was smarter to call than walk over and walk back mission unaccomplished.

I didn't get up from the glider. I just waited for whomever to appear at the top of the deck stairs. It was Fletcher.

"Thank you for accepting my roses." He sat on the little ice cream chair across from the glider.

"They're very beautiful. Thank you." It seemed an appropriate thing to say though an inner trembling had begun. I asked, "Would you care for a cup of tea?" I had made a large pot, after all. He seemed more contrite than threatening.

He indicated he would like tea. "Do you take cream or sugar?" I was standing to go in to get him a mug.

"No, no, plain is fine."

"It's not really plain. It has orange and spices in it and is quite tasty."

He said, "I thought it smelled better than regular tea. I don't need anything in it." I took two steps inside the kitchen door and reached into the cupboard for a mug. I was half worried he'd follow me but he sat as still as stone until I handed him the mug full of tea. He took a sip. "This is really good. I'll have to check it out next time I go to Safeway."

We just sat there; me on the glider, he on the little yellow chair drinking our tea. There was absolute silence. It seemed as though even the birds were holding their breaths. After more than 20 minutes passed, he set his mug on the table by the chair and stood up.

"Thank you very much for the tea. I enjoyed it very much." It appeared he was leaving. I wasn't going to breathe a sigh of relief though until he was gone. I hadn't heard his truck so have no idea where he had parked.

I stood up also and said, "Thank you for the roses. Isn't it hard to get such perfect roses in the winter?"

"I don't know," he said. "I leave it up to the florist." And with that he turned and left.

I went inside immediately—locking the kitchen door behind me—and went to the picture window in the living room. There was a small bank of snow against the house. There were footprints in the snow. He had looked in the living room window before he came around back. He saw the roses on the coffee table. Was that why he was so polite?

Much of Summit Ridge isn't visible from this window. I went to the second bedroom and looked out that window. His truck was just beginning to move. He had parked more than 100 yards up Summit Ridge from the house almost in front of the Bayhs. The truck is so big that he couldn't turn around on the narrow road though it appeared that was what he had wanted to do. He ended up backing up the Ridge. There's a turnaround area where Summit Ridge meets Wade Lane. That's a lot of backing. Why didn't he want me to know he was there? If he hadn't seen the roses would he have left? Hmmm.

I went back out on the deck and gathered up the tea mugs and pot. So much for a quiet afternoon. Well, actually, it wasn't so bad. No altercation; no wild outburst. I just hope that it is not a sign of things to come. I don't need Fletcher Ellison sitting on my back deck very often. Once was enough.

Chapter Twelve

Jack and Carrie got back late Sunday afternoon. Charles called me and also had left a message for them on their answering machine. He had bought some very large, very fresh scallops. Could we come for dinner around 7? I told him I had bought some incredible Riesling last week. Could I bring it to serve with dinner? Charles was delighted. He had everything he needed for his recipe but no wine for dinner and hadn't wanted to go out. About 7, I took 2 bottles of wine and crossed the street. Carrie and Jack were just coming out their front door so I waited for them. Charles and Mary are most gracious and started us off with a pre-dinner martini. It was nearly 11 o'clock when we all staggered home. Two martinis before dinner; two bottles of wine with dinner and some wild after dinner drink that Charles had dreamed up for the occasion.

I was surprised to wake up at my usual 6:30 without a hangover. We seldom get together on a Sunday night as three of us do work. I saw Jack leave as usual at 7:30—perhaps we hadn't had too much to drink after all.

My mother had called last evening while I was out and left a message that she and Daddy have decided they should come to Payson for Christmas. No sense in all of us being alone. I called her back just before leaving for work, about 8:30. Did they want me to come get them? No, Daddy thinks he's capable of the drive—even if it snows. What day would they be here? Thursday. What time should they leave to get here about the time I get home? We discussed all the logistics of the trip and their stay.

Now, I need to buy a Christmas tree. There is a large picture window at the west end of my living room. It overlooks the side, uncovered, deck. I can switch the chair and large end table around. The tree would fit on the end table if I bought a small tree. For the life of me, I can't remember where there is a tree lot. Safeway sells trees but they've been standing in the parking lot for weeks. I don't really have the time to get a permit and go looking for one in the wilderness either. I'll ask at work. Or ask Carrie. She and Jack brought home a tree last week.

The day seemed to plod along. We're getting off early on Thursday and it seems as though each of us can hardly wait for the end of the week. And next week will be short because of New Year's. 1980 is nearly over. Seems incredible that I would be here, in Payson, alone. Just a few years ago we bought the house for vacations with the ultimate goal of retiring here. Here I am, 40 years old, still working and alone.

I need to stay away from such dark thoughts and memories and know it. With a bit of effort I let them go and by day's end I was delighted my parents were coming for Christmas. Maybe I can convince them to stay through the end of the year. But, they're both so active in their Senior Centers they probably have some big New Year's thing planned.

I wasn't home more than half an hour when Carrie came knocking at my door. She was on her way home—in fact, her car was parked in front of my mail box on the street. Unusual.

"Come in." I pushed open the storm door so she could get in. "What's up?"

"News." She said. "Big news. And I couldn't wait to tell you."

"You're pregnant?" That was only big news I could think of.

"Good lord, no." Carrie took off her mittens.

"Well, come in and sit down. Take off your coat and tell me what's new." I took her coat and hung it on one of the hooks George had put behind the door. She stepped out of her galoshes. No snow on the ground but everything is kind of mushy.

"I was just brewing some tea. It's probably steeped by now. Care for a cup?" I headed toward the kitchen.

"Yes, please." She sat down and I pulled out a tray to set the tea pot and mugs on. Like me, Carrie drinks her tea neat. No need for spoons, sugar or milk. I sat the tray on the low table in front of the couch and poured two mugs of steaming hot tea.

"Okay. What's up?" I sat at the opposite end of the couch with my feet tucked under me. "I don't believe I've seen you this excited since the day you signed the final papers on the house."

"Well, you know how Fletcher is always after you and you said that even if you like him you wouldn't give him the time of day because he's married?" She paused for a breath.

I nodded.

"He's not married." Carrie took a sip of her tea. "While Mary Ellen was at lunch today, he asked me why you were so aloof and wouldn't speak to him most of the time. I told him it's because he's married." Another sip of tea. "And he said, "No, I'm not. My wife and I divorced a year or so ago. Get my personal file and I'll show you the paperwork." So I went to the file room to get his file. There's a personal file, a real estate file, and a couple other that are tabbed Fletcher Ellison. So I pulled the personal file and brought it out to him. Eleanor. I saw the paperwork. She filed for divorce and he was served last June. He says everything is final except the property settlement. She's being a bit hard about that because everything was hers when they married and she believes he doesn't deserve one single thing."

I was amazed that Carrie recited this as she did. Of course, he deserves nothing. Should I say so and have Carrie upset with me or do I let her go on as if Fletcher was the underdog in a bad divorce? She sounded like a junior high kid.

"Carrie, stop and think about it. What actually does Fletcher deserve? If everything belonged to Mrs. Ellison before they were married, shouldn't everything belong to her after the marriage is over?" I studied my tea mug waiting for an answer.

It took quite a few seconds before she looked at me and said, "Of course, you're right. Why should he get something that wasn't his in the first place." She shook her head and took another sip of tea. "What planet was I on this afternoon?"

"You work for Fletcher. And he can smooze so well that I am sure he made it sound like he was being cheated out of something." I reached for the tea pot to add some hot to my mug. "He's in a line of work where it is to his advantage to help people believe his client is innocent; or her property should be his or whatever. Don't feel bad. And, it might be a good idea if you didn't voice this new idea in front of him. I am sure he can be a vicious man when crossed."

I had never told Jack and Carrie about the 'walk home' incident. Maybe I should have. But I was so ticked that I had been talked into going with him that I didn't want anyone to know how totally stupid I had been. And, because of the way I feel, I doubt that Duane will ever tell anyone. He's still apologetic about it.

"Well, regardless of property, he's not married. He really wants to get to know you." Carrie set her mug on the tray.

"And he wants you to help convince me; is that it?" I just shook my head. This is just like junior high school.

"Well, yes, sort of, I guess. He's taking Mary Ellen and her husband and Jack and I for dinner Wednesday evening. It's our last work day until after Christmas. He wants you to come along."

He had really gotten to her. Now she is feeling like an idiot. I am laying odds he actually asked her to ask me to go with them.

"When are you supposed to let him know if I'll go or not?" I figured—what the hell; at this point I may as well get it out and over with.

She looked at me with big wide eyes. "How did you know I was supposed to ask you?"

"Carrie, it's just his style. Not to worry. You can go in tomorrow and tell him you told me he's single and you asked about dinner and I said that I couldn't make it. My parents are coming for Christmas." Now I'm acting like a junior high kid. Blame it on the parents.

"Oh, really, your folks are coming? That's great. My folks want us to come down to the valley. I would love a white Christmas and it sure won't happen in Mesa." She looked relieved.

"It might not happen here either, kiddo. Payson doesn't get that much snow. There have been winters that the old timers will tell you about but overall Payson doesn't get that much snow."

"Jack thinks we should go down for Christmas and have a party on New Year's. What do you think? Do you have plans for New Year's?"

Suddenly I realized that I would be alone for the coming of the New Year. George and I used to have such wonderful times on New Year's Eve. The idea of it was too much and a tear ran down my nose and dropped with a small plop into my mug.

Carrie looked up and realized there were a couple more tears falling. "Oh, Eleanor, I am so sorry. I didn't mean to make you sad. We could invite all the neighbors and have a great party. It wouldn't be a substitute for George but we could have a good party. I know we could."

I fumbled in my sweater pocket for a tissue. Blowing my nose I told her, "It's okay, Carrie. I just get sad sometimes. And the holidays are so hard because we enjoyed them so much. His kids, my kids, my folks, the neighbors, the church choir—there was something going on almost daily from mid-December through New Year's Day. You have the New Year's Eve party and I'll have the New Year's Day bash. How's that sound?"

She slid across the middle cushion of the couch and put her arm around my shoulders. "That sounds like a great plan."

I didn't want to shake her off but her hug didn't make it any better. I stood up and said, "Okay. Now New Year's Day we start off with cinnamon rolls and hot chocolate while we watch the Rose Parade. There is a buffet laid out around 11 and everyone eats at will during the numerous football games. Supper is late; depending on the last ball game. It's also quite simple. Plenty to eat and drink all day but nothing outrageously fancy. Deal?"

This was the New Year's Day George and I had spent for 15 years. There was a flow of people in and out all day. Some came to watch a particular ball game. Some came to eat and talk. New Year's Day was a people day. But until a few minutes ago, I hadn't given it a thought.

Carrie pulled her galoshes on. "I had better get home. Jack's due any minute. Just remember—Fletcher Ellison is not married. Okay? Oh, and guess what Fletcher gave me today?"

"What?"

"A bottle of Emeraude! He said he understood that was my favorite fragrance."

I opened the door for her and watched as she pulled on her mittens while walking to the car. Did I really care that Fletcher wasn't married? Not on your life. I wondered if it made a difference to Carrie? I hoped not. And as for the Emeraude—could I have dropped my list in the driveway and he picked it up? Or does he just have a very good nose for fragrances?

Chapter Thirteen

After Carrie left, I sat on the couch with my mug gripped firmly in my hands. I haven't had a lot of melancholy since George's death. I've worked at not being maudlin. But the sudden thought of New Year's Eve was just too much. I returned my tea mug to the tray and stood up to take everything back into the kitchen. Suddenly the tears just flowed. I laid down on the couch and cried. Time flew by without notice until I realized it was almost dark in the house. I wiped my nose and took the tray of tea things into the kitchen.

Where are my Christmas decorations? I am sure they were moved with everything else. Probably in the garage. I took a flashlight out of the kitchen drawer, pulled on a heavy sweater and went out to the garage. At the bottom of the deck stairs, next to the garage door, were footprints in the slush. I hadn't come in this way this afternoon. And the footprints were much larger than my size 5s. Closer investigation showed mud traces on the deck steps. Someone was on my deck today some time! The path by the garage to the deck doesn't get any sun until late afternoon. Slush comes from heat on old snow—so someone was here just before I got home or maybe even after Carrie left.

I stepped over the footprints carefully, unlocked the garage and went in. Once inside, I turned on the interior garage light. It was still rather dim and I used my flashlight to light the boxes on the shelves. While packing, I had labeled every box. At the end of the first shelf sat two boxes marked "Xmas Stuff". The shelf was low enough I could reach up and slide the boxes forward and lower them to the garage floor. I couldn't remember having two boxes of Christmas stuff until I opened one and found it full of outdoor lights and stuff to put up on the outside of the house. The other box had tree ornaments, garlands and centerpieces—stuff like that. I put the outdoor box back. No way was I going to try to decorate the house outside at this late date.

The indoor box was good-sized and fairly heavy. George had a brother-in-law who was a butcher and every so often he would give me a waxed chicken box. He'd rinse it well and I only knew it was a chicken box because that's what the outside marking said. "Fresh California Chickens". Because the box was waxed inside and out, it was waterproof if you put the lid on securely. Perfect for storing things you use once a year.

I sat the box on the deck at the top of the stairs and relocked the garage door. That task irritated me no end. Payson is supposed to be a peaceful community where you can leave your house unlocked. It used to be that way.

The box was dusty so I sat it on the little round table on the deck and turned on the deck light to see what I needed to do as clean up. After I had the box dusted and decent, I brought it into the living room and sat it on the table in front of the couch. I steeled myself for the opening. I was sure there'd be a flood of memories I couldn't deal with now. But, I have to have the tree up and decorated by the time my parents arrive Thursday. It would be nice to do the entire house; as we used to do.

Item by item, I unloaded the box. Garlands, centerpieces, tree ornaments, even a new box of tinsel. I choked up a bit. George was a tinsel fanatic. It had to be laid on each branch, just so.

Once the box of decorations was sorted I decided that I could actually use everything laying on the couch and table. I took the box back to the garage and put it back on the shelf, empty. I looked at the footprints again at the bottom of the steps. They pointed toward the deck.

After locking the garage again, I crossed over the deck to the small uncovered deck on the west end of the house. There were footsteps in the half melted snow. It seemed to me from the prints that someone had stood at the living room picture window before exiting the deck through the front yard. I wish I knew when these prints were made. I wish.

Back inside I decided the decorating could wait until tomorrow. My stomach growled a bit and I realized I hadn't eaten dinner yet. It was nearly 9pm. I puttered around in the kitchen and heated some soup and made a grilled cheese sandwich. Darn—no milk. I found a can of soda and went to the family room to eat. The light from the lamps in the living room gave a dim but rosy glow in the family room and I decided I needed no more light than that.

When I finished, I called Jack and Carrie's house. "Sorry to bug you at this hour, but where did you buy your Christmas tree?"

Jack evidently turned to ask Carrie as his voice was slightly muffled, "Hon, where did we get the tree?" She said something I couldn't make out and he came back to the phone. Carrie says we got it at 84 Lumber. I was just along to tote and carry so I am sure she's right. $12.50 for a 5 foot tree."

"Thanks, Jack. My folks will be here Thursday and I absolutely have to have a tree up and decorated." He made some small talk about parents and traditions and we hung up.

Although it wasn't all that late suddenly I was exhausted. I made sure everything was locked up and turned off. While in the shower I thought I heard the telephone ring. "Well, too bad. Leave a message." I thought to myself. I had completely forgotten my resolve to disconnect the answering machine.

I was brushing my teeth a few minutes later and heard the phone—for sure this time. I picked up the bedroom extension. "Hello." No answer. I said, "Hello" one more time. Still no response though the line sounds open. A bit peeved I said, "If you don't want to talk to me, you shouldn't call. It's just that simple." I hung up the phone.

I finished brushing my teeth and went to bed. It could not have taken more than two minutes before I was sound asleep.

The next morning I realized there was a message on my answering machine. Evidently from the night before—while I was in the shower. But, as usually, there was no one there. I erased it.

I dawdled around cleaning the tree ornaments after breakfast until I realized I would be late for work if I didn't leave almost immediately. How time flies! The sun was shining and no expectation of snow or rain so I didn't bother with galoshes; just my gloves and coat. I got to work just as Anne drove up; I wasn't late after all. She was surprised to see me as usually I have the coffee on by the time she arrives.

"I was sorting tree ornaments and making sure they were shiny," I offered an explanation before she asked. "My parents are coming for Christmas and I haven't bought a tree yet."

She used her key to open the office door. "We bought ours at 84 Lumber this year. Seems very fresh and smells great. And the price was right."

Second recommendation for the same place-that's a good sign. I have early lunch today so I think I'll go buy a Christmas tree.

The day quickly settled into a leisurely pace. Not too many escrows closing the week of Christmas. But Duane said there would be a little flurry right after New Year's. "There always is," he said. "I don't know if people make resolutions to get a vacation home or if it's their present to themselves. But we usually have escrow work in early January."

When I was ready to go to lunch I announced to anyone listening that I was buying a Christmas tree on my lunch hour but would be back as usual. Jim, who would be leaving at noon, said, "You'd better be. I am meeting a friend for lunch." I waved at him and left, humming some Christmas ditty.

When I got to the Christmas tree lot I spotted "my" tree almost immediately. It is about 3 feet tall. I am putting it on a low table in front of the window; the size was perfect. I paid the $8 and put the tree in the trunk. How incredible, I couldn't believe finding a perfect tree almost immediately. George and I used to spend hours selecting a tree. I came home the back way—Wade Lane to Summit. As I came down the Ridge I saw Fletcher's truck parked in my driveway. I parked to the left of it—what the hell is he doing here?

I took the tree out of the trunk and came around the garage to the deck steps. As I reached the top step, I was confronted by Fletcher—he was obviously upset. "Why are you so late? You should have been home 20 minutes ago."

"What are you talking about? I am not on a schedule. As far as I am concerned I am exactly on time." I set the tree by the kitchen door.

It was then I realized there was food on my little outdoor table. "What's this?" I asked as I took off my gloves.

"I thought it would be a nice surprise for me to provide lunch for you today." He eased back just a tad.

"Fletcher, why?"

"Well, I knew you wouldn't meet me somewhere for lunch if I called and asked. So I just brought lunch to you. You usually come home on Tuesdays."

"Well, I'm here. But I don't have a lot of time. I don't know why you think you can just intrude on my life." I slipped out of my coat. The noonday sun was hitting the deck and, beside that, I was hot under the collar.

"Please, Eleanor, sit down and have a bit of lunch. You still have almost half an hour. You don't have to do anything but eat." He pulled one of the chairs away from the table.

The lunch spread looked very appetizing. I don't know why I sat down. I guess it's easier than arguing with him. "Thank you." I was referring to the chair pull but I'm not sure he understood that.

He had opened the containers so the salads, cheese and bread was visible. He had a bottle of wine too. "Fletcher, I can't accept a drink. I need to return to work in half an hour." He looked a bit disgusted but put the bottle in a bag sitting on the deck by the table.

"Okay, I have a bottle of water and a bottle of soda. Which do you prefer?"

"What brand soda?" I don't drink a lot of soda so have become quite choosey about what I do drink.

He held up a bottle. Of course, it would be my favorite. "Thank you." I said again. He poured a plastic cup full and handed it to me. I helped myself to some salad and cheese. He sat down across from me and I handed him the containers. He broke a piece of bread off the loaf and offered me the rest. I took a small piece and returned the loaf to its long paper sleeve.

I was hungry; I was in a hurry. I wasn't overly enthusiastic about this lunch. I said nothing but ate quickly. He ate at a more leisurely pace and watched me closely. I was getting a little riled again.

Finally, when it appeared I had finished he asked, "Did Carrie tell you that I am divorced and available?"

"Yes, she did. Last evening on her way home from work. Tell me Fletcher, why doesn't anyone in town know about your divorce?" I don't think that was asking too much.

He seemed surprised at the question though. Finally, he stammered, "My wife, my ex-wife, doesn't want anyone to know. Her religion frowns on divorce."

"Isn't her religion the same as yours?" I finished my soda.

"Well, yes, but I don't see everything exactly the same way she, and the church, sees things."

"Fletcher, isn't it a matter of tenet? How can you dismiss certain parts of the faith just because you don't agree with it? That is difficult for me to understand." I looked at my watch and stood up.

He realized I was getting ready to leave. "Eleanor, don't go back to work. We really need to talk."

I put my coat over my arm. I'd need it coming home this evening. "Jimmy has a date for lunch and he can't leave until I get back. I'm sorry, Fletcher, but your talk is going to have to wait." I picked up my purse and started backing toward the stairs. I didn't trust him enough to turn my back on him.

"When? When can we talk?" He was still seated. I backed a few more feet.

"Well, I don't know. My parents are coming up for Christmas and things are going to be a bit hectic the next few days. Can this wait until next week?" I kept backing up. He was still seated.

"All right. I'll call you tonight around 8 and maybe we can set a date; just to talk." I was almost to the top of the stairs and had to raise my voice.

"If you're calling tonight, why can't we just talk then?"

He didn't have an answer. I turned, ran down the stairs and got into the car. I was out of the driveway before he got around the garage. I cannot believe I just had lunch with Fletcher Ellison on my own deck. I never got into the house. I hope he didn't either.

I am not looking forward to his call this evening. I have to decorate the house; set up the tree; wrap packages. Not only do I not want to talk to him; I don't really have the time.

It was one minute to the end of my hour when I walked into the office. Jimmy was standing there with his coat on. "I was beginning to think you were going to be late."

"Jimmy, you have no idea what an excruciating hour this has been for me. I was beginning to think I wouldn't get back—period." I hung my coat on the rack by the front door. He was already gone. Hope his lunch goes better than mine.

Chapter Fourteen

The rest of the day actually seemed to fly by. Lots of little chores to complete before the holiday kept me busy right up to 4:30. Duane came in and asked if I'd mind making the deposit tonight as he had let Anne go home earlier. I hadn't even missed her. Wow! I guess I was busier than I thought. But of course, I would make the deposit.

The bank drive through lane was empty and I was home before 5. I parked in the driveway and went around to the deck door. I unlocked the door before I suddenly realized my three foot tree was gone and there was a six footer in its place. What is this?

I went into the house and checked the phone book. I called Fletcher's office. Carrie answered the phone. "Is he there?" I asked her very calmly.

"Yes. Hold on a moment." She put me on hold and a moment later Fletcher picked up the phone.

"Fletcher, where is my Christmas tree?" I was working to keep my voice level.

"Well, Ellie, Sweetie, it was right there on the deck when I left." He sounded very jolly. I think he may have had a client in his office.

"Fletcher, where is my three foot tree? I bought it especially to put on a low table in front of a window in the living room. I have no place for a six foot tree. Where is my little tree?" I maintained an even tone.

"I am sorry, Sweetie. I thought I was doing you a favor. I brought the little one back to the office. We are going to decorate it tomorrow." He definitely had a client in the office. He was being too syrupy.

"Fletcher, how long will you be in the office?"

"Well, I have a client here. I'll be in the office at least half an hour." I knew he had a client. He was playacting for someone.

"Thank you." I hung up.

69

I wrestled the big tree into my trunk and fastened the lid with a bungee cord. My poor car doesn't deserve the way I drove it down the Ridge. I pulled in front of Fletcher's office. His car, Carrie's car and another car were parked in front. I heaved the tree out of the trunk and walked it to the door. Carrie saw me coming and opened the door.

"Here's Fletcher's office tree, Carrie. Where's my tree?" She pointed to a bay window; the tree was leaning against the wall. I picked up my tree and left. I was furious. Not at Carrie. I am sure she didn't have a clue where he got the little tree. I am sure she didn't know he'd left me a replacement. But I was angry anyhow. Not at Carrie but with the man for whom she worked. Furious is a better description. I was extremely angry.

I put my tree back in the trunk. On the way home I stopped at Pioneer Market and bought some more tinsel. It was on sale. I am not a strand by strand tinsel placer . . . I need a lot of tinsel to decorate a tree.

When I got home, the phone was ringing. "Hello." I was a bit out of breath running to catch it before it went to the answering machine. It was Fletcher.

"You're angry with me, aren't you?" What a stupid question!

"What gives you that idea, Mr. Ellison?" Here I go again, pussyfooting around him. He scares me. The lunch was creepy; the tree thing even worse.

"I am sorry. I honestly thought perhaps you couldn't afford a big tree and I was just trying to be helpful. I am sorry. Honest." He sounded sorry.

"Mr. Ellison, I appreciate the lunch today. I appreciate your misguided tree trade. But I wish you wouldn't try to be so helpful without talking to me about it first. My parents are coming and I would like them to enjoy the visit. Please, will you leave me alone?" I was ready to cry but tried to not let that show in my voice.

"Eleanor, I want to be your friend. I think we'd make a good team. You're stubborn and I'm persistent. That's a good mix. I realize we've gotten off on the wrong foot—more than once. Forgive me and allow me to make it up to you." He sounded too sincere for my liking.

I realized I was gripping the telephone very tightly. My mind was racing. Calm down. Calm down. Tell him to buzz off calmly.

"Mr. Ellison, please don't try to make up anything. You have no idea how you have traumatized me. You can have no idea how to make it up to me. Please, just leave me alone. Please." I hung up the telephone.

I went back to the deck and brought in my tree. It is a beautiful and well-shaped long needled pine. It's pretty thickly branched and I can hardly wait to get it up and decorated. I had put the tree stand on the kitchen sink last night so it would be ready. I moved the easy chair to one side and realigned the octagon shaped end table under the window. I put down a newspaper and set the stand on the table. When I had it in the middle of the picture window, I filled the tree stand with sugar water then fitted the tree into it gently. I don't have to trim anything. It is a perfect fit. And, I can reach the top of the tree with no problem.

I closed the drapes in both the dining and living rooms. I decided to have some dinner before getting involved in decorating the tree. The front door bell rang. It had better not be Fletcher.

It was Carrie. "Are you just getting home from work?" I asked her as I let her in.

"We had a client until after 5 and Fletcher asked me to wait until he called you. He wanted to give me his client notes tonight as he won't be in in the morning. But, he really wanted to talk to you. What the heck is going on?" The way she asked, I am glad I haven't blamed her for anything. Obviously she doesn't have a clue what her boss has been up to.

"It started at lunch time, Carrie. Want some wine? I've just opened a bottle of chardonnay." I didn't wait for any answer; I just got down two glasses and poured. "I bought this tree on my lunch hour. I came home and Fletcher was on the back deck with lunch spread on the deck table. He insists we have to talk and he was upset because I was late. Of course I was late—I stopped and bought a tree. When I left to go back to work, my three-foot tree was on the deck by the kitchen door and your boss was sitting at my table finishing his lunch.

"When I came home tonight there was a six foot tree on my deck by the kitchen door and no sign of your boss anywhere."

"Oh, brother. I knew I shouldn't have passed your call to him when you called this evening. As the client left she made some comment about it and he said not to worry—just a lover's quarrel." Carrie took a long drink of wine.

"What? He's a jackass. What is he trying to do to my reputation? What is trying to do to me?" I sat down and stared at the tree. "I don't want you to worry about this, Carrie. Somehow, I'll handle it. I asked him this afternoon to leave me alone; I don't want him spoiling my folk's visit."

She finished her wine and got up. "I've got to get home. If you need anything, call." I promised I would and locked the door behind her.

What next? I guess I'll find out as the week unfolds.

I went back to the kitchen and finished putting together a quick dinner. A tree is waiting for me to trim it and I have been looking forward to it. My boohoos of last night have helped put me in a better mood. Yes, sometimes crying can make you feel better. It'll be the first tree I've trimmed alone in lot of years. The tinsel may not be perfectly placed but the tree will be perfect anyhow.

Chapter Fifteen

Seven white roses were delivered to the office the next afternoon. They were arranged in a white vase with fir boughs and a red ribbon. While very pretty, I didn't want them on my desk. The card said "You must allow me to do things for you. Fletcher". I asked Cyndi if she had room on the reception desk so that everyone could enjoy the roses. She was delighted.

Jack and Carrie are going to her parents for Christmas so I invited them to dinner on Thursday so they could meet my parents. Dad and Mom feel a lot better now that they know I have such good neighbors. They all got along quite well. Carrie had knit a sweater for me that she insist I open after dinner. I had knit matching caps, scarves and mittens for the two of them.

We had a bottle of wine and some munchies while everyone remembered other Christmases in other places. It was really quite pleasant. 'Til now, in every telephone conversation I've had with my mother she would complain "It's too soon for you to make such important decisions. You shouldn't move to Payson and be alone." I have a feeling those conversations are a thing of the past.

Christmas Eve Mom, Dad and I went to the candlelight service. While we were in church a light snow had fallen. We went home in good humor and Dad regaled us with stories I've heard a hundred times about the snowstorms they suffered through in Minnesota when he was a boy. We had some hot chocolate and talked into the wee hours.

Breakfast was late on Christmas Day. But, tradition requires we don't eat lunch at all and dinner is after 3 pm, so eating breakfast later is better. I am never sure if it's a late lunch, and early dinner, or just Christmas dinner. The ham is in the oven. I put the potatoes in the oven about 2:45 and put the rolls on a baking sheet ready for later baking. Everything else is ready. Dad's out on the deck. He loves the view. Mother is looking through a photo album I found packed with the Christmas ornaments. It's Christmas last year.

"Who's this with George? I know I've met him but just can't remember." I ran back and forth between Mom and Dad for an hour. Finally I said that I should get the table set. "Do you need any help, Eleanor?" Mother was ready to lay the album aside.

"No, Mom, I'm fine. Everything is about ready. I just have to set the table and put the rolls in the oven." I had three china settings and the silverware out. I wanted Christmas placemats and remembered that I had stored them in the hall linen closet. While I had my head buried in the closet, the door bell rang.

Mother called out, "Shall I answer the door?" I yelled back that she should. I had located the placemats when I heard the voice . . . Fletcher Ellison. Mother came down the hall to me. "There's a Mr. Ellison here, Eleanor."

"That's Carrie's boss, Mom. Invite him in." I pulled out the entire tissue wrapped bundle of Christmas placemats and went back to the dining room. I couldn't believe that he'd show up today. He knew my family would be here.

"Fletcher, Carrie and Jack have gone to the valley for the day." Maybe he had intended to go there and found them not at home.

"Oh, I know. Carrie told me Thursday." He's still standing in the doorway; with the door open.

"Well," I hesitated. "Come in. Mother, this is Fletcher Ellison. He's Carrie Bayh's boss. You may remember her mentioning him at dinner."

"Oh, yes, indeed." Mother fluttered a bit. "Can you stay for dinner, Mr. Ellison? Eleanor is just setting the table now."

I wondered if Fletcher was hoping for dinner or if he just lucked out. But, either way, Mother has invited him. "Yes, Fletcher, take off your coat and stay for dinner." It was then I realized he had his hands full. A large bottle of wine, a larger box of candy and a couple small, gaily wrapped packages. He handed me the wine and candy and set the packages on the table in front of the couch.

He removed his coat and looked around. Maybe he never has been in this house before. I sort of pointed toward the coat hooks behind the door. Just then my Dad came in. "How soon is dinner, Sister?" He was surprised to see Fletcher standing in the living room. "I'm sorry; didn't know we had company."

"Dad, this is Fletcher Ellison. He's Carrie's boss. Mother has just invited him to dinner. Which, by the way, is almost ready." I handed Dad the bottle of wine. "Fletcher brought some wine for dinner." I didn't realize at that moment that it almost sounded like Fletcher had been invited. I hoped Dad knew better.

Fletcher spoke up. "I hope it's appropriate for the meal."

My Dad said, "Who cares what color a wine is if it's a good wine?" He looked at the label. "This is a good wine, indeed. Sister, where's the corkscrew?" He followed me into the kitchen and I fished a corkscrew out of the drawer. At the same time I got another setting of silver and china and 4 wine glasses.

When we were finally at the table; Dad at one end, Mother at the other, I said. "Besides being an attorney, Mr. Ellison is also an ordained minister. Fletcher will you lead us in thanks for dinner?"

He looked at me rather surprised. Either he didn't know I knew or he didn't think I'd bring it up. But, he prayed a passable prayer.

The wine was very good. I discovered that Fletcher can be witty and charming and tell only funny jokes when he wants. We were at the table an hour and a half before we got to the pies.

Fletcher left the house around 8 pm. I had not opened the little gifts on the table in front of the couch. Hopefully, Mother wouldn't make an issue of them. She had opened the candy after dinner and passed it around as a final sweet to a marvelous meal. At least, I think that's what she said. I was getting a bit fidgety by then. The man makes me nervous. I don't feel good around him.

After he was gone my Mother proclaimed he is 'a very pleasant man' and she liked him. My Dad isn't so sure. God bless Dad.

Chapter Sixteen

Dad and Mom left two days after Christmas. They have big doings at two different Senior Centers in Mesa for New Year's. They seemed to enjoy their visit in Payson a lot. As they left though, my Dad said, "There's something about that Ellison fellow that I'd be wary of if I was you."

I told Dad that I was already wary of him. I asked, "You do know that he invited himself over for Christmas, don't you?" Dad said he thought as much as I had some fine Riesling in the fridge and had set the table for three originally.

"Well, regardless, you were gracious and we enjoyed the day." Leave it to my Dad to see the good side of anything.

Jack and Carrie got back the night before we had to return to work. They had a great time in the valley; went to a major concert and did a few other things they couldn't do in Payson. We got together on my back deck to plan New Year's. I had no one coming from out of town but a number of Jack's friends were coming. He said he and some of his pals want to schedule some bike rides in the next couple months so he said he suggested they take their holiday time and come up for New Year's and enjoy the peace and quiet of his new home town.

Then Jack started to panic about where all his friends would sleep. I reminded him that I have 2 unused bedrooms—a queen size bed in one and a single in the other. Some of his friends are welcome to stay at my house.

We decided that we'd work together on both New Year's Eve and New Year's Day. Food, activities, sleeping arrangements. In a couple hours and a fair quantity of wine later we had everything planned. I have my list of things I need to buy and provide. I'd better start on it right after work tomorrow. The week between Christmas and New Years is terribly short! We decided to invite everyone on the Ridge in winter residence. Charles and Mary live here year round; but Sam and Stella, next door to Charles, probably won't be back until Easter. Up the Ridge from Jack and Carrie's there are 3 couples who are year round residents. That would be a nice manageable group even if everyone came. Jack is pretty sure 7 of his friends are coming. So probably eighteen people in all. I am very comfortable with that and so is Carrie.

The office is slow. Duane told us we could each take an hour and a half for lunch; only two people need to be in the office at a time this week. Good news for me. I would rather shop and come out to daylight. I started filling my party supply list at lunch the next day.

On Thursday I took down my Christmas tree and all the decorations in the house except the garlands. I cleaned and wrapped everything and repacked it carefully in the chicken box. I set the box on the dryer so that it would be handy when I want to take down and store the garlands.

New Year's Eve Day Jack's friends began arriving at Jack's before 5pm. They were sitting on the Bayh's deck when I got home. Evidently they all got off work early. I don't know any of them so just went into my own house.

Carrie was home first. She called me right away and asked if it was okay to send one couple over now. There's a single guy coming later that she'd like to house with me also. I said, "Sure. Who are they? Tell them to come to the front door."

She told me that Ron and Donna Bello were on their way down. Ron used to work with Jack before she and Jack moved to Arizona. He and Jack still ride their motorcycles together.

I opened the front door and welcomed two really friendly people. They were enthused that neighbors could be so accommodating. I showed them my second bedroom and explained that they would share a bath with the other bedroom. They could see no problem in that.

I love this house for the bathrooms. I have a master bath and then a guest bath between the two front bedrooms. Well, actually, I love this house for a lot of things—the decks, the freestanding fireplace in the family room; the dishwasher; the picture windows. Heck, I just love the house.

They brought in their luggage and then Ron and Donna went back to the Bayhs. I told them I wouldn't lock the door at night but the last one in should.

I was midway through dinner when there was a knock on the front door. It was Jack's single friend, Dennis. He introduced himself and apologized for not waiting for Jack to call me. I told him it was no problem. "Come on in and I'll show you your room." I explained the shared bath and the open door for the weekend. "Have you eaten? I am still at the dinner table if you care to join me."

"Hey, that's great. I think they've finished dinner at Jack's though Carrie said she could whip something for me."

"I'll call her and tell her you're eating with me tonight." I went to the telephone and when Carrie answered said, "Don't worry about dinner for Dennis. He's eating with me."

She was grateful and said to send him back when he was ready. Dennis said he'd be just a minute. He wanted to change clothes and wash up. He came straight from work.

"That is some highway getting here." Dennis was telling me about the deer and narrow highway, the slow tractor that trapped him for 10 miles and more deer.

"The Beeline is not the best highway in the world. There's rumor that a lot of it will be 2 lanes each way in the next few years . . . especially through Slate Creek." I passed the casserole back to him.

He looked at me. "Do you want anymore of this or may I finish it?"

"Please, finish it." I passed the sliced tomatoes too. It'd definitely be easier for the weekend if the fridge isn't full of leftovers.

About half an hour after Dennis had helped me rinse the dishes and put them into the dishwasher, he said he was going back to the Bayh's. "Want to come along?" He asked me.

"Thanks but I have a lot of stuff to do for tomorrow's shindig. Have a good time. As I told Ron and Donna—the last to come in should turn off the porch light and lock the door if I have already gone to bed." He said he'd do that and slipped into his jacket and went next door. I did lock the kitchen door to the deck.

I cleaned veggies and made sauces and bar-b-qued beef. About 11, I decided I absolutely had to go to bed. It was understood that Jack's friends would go to Jack's for meals tomorrow but if anyone is here when I am ready to eat, I'll invite them.

The telephone rang about midnight. There was a lamp on in each bedroom and the porch light was on when I went to bed. The deck light hasn't been on all night. Are we getting back to late night calls? I was ticked.

Because of the call, I was awake when Jack's friends came in an hour later. They were quiet and lights were out in about fifteen minutes. This isn't so bad. I wanted to check that the front door was locked but saw the bedroom doors were open—I could disturb them stumbling around in the dark so I just rolled over and finally got back to sleep.

The end of the year is here. I can't say I am sad to see 1980 go. There have been so many ups and downs—it'll be good to start anew.

Chapter Seventeen

I was nearly asleep again when I heard a shout. It was from inside the house. I jumped out of bed and grabbed my robe on the run. Ron and Donna were in the bedroom next to me. Their door was open; they were sitting up and evidently had also heard the shout. I passed the bathroom in the hall that opens into both guest bedrooms. The front bedroom door was open and as I got to it someone knocked me down and ran out the front door.

Dennis was crumpled at the foot of the bed. I ran to him. "Are you okay? Who was that? What's going on?" Meanwhile, Ron was down the hall and out the front door. His robe was flying behind him. He was chasing after whoever had knocked down both Dennis and me.

Donna and I were able to help Dennis up onto his bed. He shook his head. "I was in the bathroom and as I came back into the bedroom I saw some one leaning over the bed. I hadn't turned on the light; the nightlight in the bathroom is pretty bright so whoever it was didn't realize I was behind him now."

Ron came back in. I yelled to him, "Call the police. The phone's in the dining room. We are at 713 Summit." Then I realized he wouldn't know the telephone number for the PD and called that to him as well.

Dennis had quite a bruise developing on his jaw but he said he felt okay. I went to the hall closet and found an ice bag. He thought that would help. In a few minutes, the ice bag was filled and on his jaw and Payson PD was at the front door.

They talked to Ron first as he had done the chase. They sent an officer to the area when Ron thought a vehicle had been parked to see if they could see any tire tracks or anything. Then the officer talked to Dennis who was able to give them estimated height and weight, and a few other details. I knew the least of all, well, next to Donna who knew nothing.

The officer that checked outside with Ron came back saying that there were fresh tracks in the thin layer of snow that had fallen earlier. "All I know for sure," he told his partner, "the tracks were made by a vehicle with dual rear wheels." I felt very faint and sat down hard.

The snow must have fallen after my guests had come in from Jack and Carrie's. There were footprints on the west deck; Ron hadn't gone there. There were tracks, a lot of them, to and from the front door. Too many tracks to make out one particular set coming or going.

I should have gotten up and checked the front door after everyone had gone to bed. The police officer was asking, "Was the house locked?" I looked at the three visitors. They looked at each other.

Dennis spoke up. "I guess not. We were asked to lock the door when we came in but I guess we all thought someone else had done it." The officer wanted to know they had come in from where, when, etc. It was nearly an hour before the police left. It was after 3 am.

"Anyone want some decaf?" I know that I do and headed for the kitchen without an immediate response. I put some cheese and crackers on a plate and set it on the coffee table in the family room. The fire in the fireplace was still a bed of hot coals and I added a bit of kindling and a log.

Dennis put on a robe and slippers; so did Donna. We're all sitting around in our nightclothes looking like a bookplate from a horror novel. The coffee smelled delicious as we all gathered round the coffee table. The apologies were fast and furious once they began. "We should have." "I forgot." "I thought."

Signaling for a timeout, I said, "It's over; it's done. No one's to blame. In a small town like Payson we all think we shouldn't have to lock our doors. I didn't start until a couple months ago myself. The police seem to think they know who the intruder is. The real question is why?"

I didn't want to tell these guests of Jack and Carrie's that I think Carrie's boss is a sicko. So when they asked why the police think they know, I simply told them "The tracks are unique. There aren't too many vehicles in the area with dual rear wheels." That satisfied them and we finally went back to bed—after 4.

The sun was shining brightly when I got up a few hours later. Both bedroom doors were closed and from the coats still hanging on the hooks, I was sure everyone was still here.

The coffee I put on this morning is not decaf. Soon the aroma had spread through the entire house. The muffins were just coming out of the oven when Dennis came out of the bathroom.

"Which smells better? The coffee or the muffins?" He asked me as if I knew.

"Personally, I prefer the coffee." I flipped the muffins into a napkin lined basket. "But the muffins do smell pretty good." The eggs were already whisked and waiting. I had cooked bacon last night for omelets this morning. I diced some onion and tomatoes and set them aside. "Your jaw doesn't look too bad this morning. Guess the ice worked."

He gingerly felt his face. "There's a bruise but it didn't swell. Doesn't hurt too much either. I don't think he had a square shot at me."

"That's good. Ready for breakfast?"

Dennis said, "Sure. What about Ron and Donna?"

"Let them sleep. This stuff will all hold and we can feed them later. What would you like in your omelet?"

"What do you put in yours?" He looked into the various bowls.

"Me? Some of everything."

"Okay, make mine like yours." He took his coffee and sat down on the family room couch.

"Would you like to eat outside, Dennis? It's really quite pleasant on the deck when the sun is out."

He opened the back door. "Hey, nice little table. Want me to bring out the silver or the placemats or something?'

I showed him where the silver was and the placemats were stacked on the counter by the sink. "Take the coffee and muffins out too, would you?" He would.

I had two sauté skillets on the stove and made both omelets at one time. I flipped them onto plates. Dennis walked back into the kitchen just at that moment and I handed both plates to him. I got the butter out of the fridge and a jar of peaches from the cupboard. We were ready to eat.

Dennis was impressed with the view and asked what's this and where does that road go and other things like that. It was a very pleasant meal. I learned that he lives and works in California. He and Jack are friends of long standing. They had worked together for nearly eighteen years before Jack and Carrie decided to move to Arizona.

Among other things, they ride motorcycles together. One thing they planned to do either tonight at the party or tomorrow between ball games was to work out a schedule for riding next year. When they all lived close together they'd decide Wednesday that they would go out on Friday or whatever. Now it took a bit of planning. But they've been doing this for a while and meet in Baker and usually go to Dumont Dunes. Ron is also from California. The other two guys that are up for the party both worked with Jack in Mesa.

My George and his friends used to ride at Dumont Dunes sometimes. But I didn't want to ask Dennis if he knew George. I don't think I could handle that right now.

I got up to take our plates in when Ron and Donna appeared at the kitchen door. "Hi, guys!" Dennis got up from his chair. "Want some breakfast? This lady makes a mean omelet. And she baked muffins. And the peaches in the jar? She canned those in August."

"Wow!" I said. "If I ever need a press agent, I know where to find one." I bowed to the left and to the right. Everyone laughed. "If Dennis will sit on the glider, there will be places for two at the breakfast table." Dennis was standing already and bowed back at me. He picked up his cup, poured some more coffee and sat on the glider. "How do you like your omelets?"

I stepped inside and got two more coffee mugs. "Anyone take cream, sugar?" No one did.

When they had told me their preferences for omelets. I went back into the kitchen and made two more and another pot of coffee. I am sure the thermos carafe is almost empty by now.

I could hear the conversation outside. Donna asked Dennis, "Does your jaw ache as badly as it looks?" I could hear her leave the chair and could imagine her touching the dark bruise on Dennis' face.

Dennis said, "No, the ice pack was a stroke of genius; no swelling and the jaw doesn't hurt much at all." I could hear Donna pull the chair out so I think she sat down again. I sautéed the bacon, onion and tomatoes quickly before adding the eggs. Omelets are simple to make with a little forethought. But they are impressive to non-cooks.

The omelets were steaming as I put them in front of Donna and Ron. Dennis was talking a mile a minute telling Ron and Donna everything I had just told him. I poured myself some more coffee and sat down next to Dennis on the glider. I live alone so there aren't too many chairs outside. The phone rang and I went inside to answer it.

It was Jack. "How is everything? Everyone up and going? Okay if we come down?

I said, "Okay. Yes. Of course." After I hung up I realized they were unaware of our middle of the night visitor. After I unlocked the front door, I took a couple of chairs out to the deck with me.

"That was Jack. I think everyone is coming over."

"Is there more coffee?" Dennis was on his feet.

"Yes, take the carafe in and fill it, if you would please." I handed him the empty coffee carafe.

And so began the last day of 1980. I am really, really, really glad to see this year go.

Chapter Eighteen

Jack and Carrie and their little group of guests came in the back way. "Coffee anyone?" Dennis had just walked out of the kitchen with the carafe. "Whoa! I should go back and get more mugs!"

I went in and got yet another pot of coffee brewing. Dennis followed me in and I showed him where the mugs were. "Oh, Dennis, I think Jack drinks cream and sugar. Hold up. Let me get both so you can take it out too." I picked a small tray from an overhead cupboard and filled it with 6 mugs, a cream pitcher and a sugar bowl. Dennis started to pick the tray. "Wait, spoons."

"This is why I drink my coffee black." Dennis winked at me and took the tray out to the deck. I pulled 2 folding chairs from the closet and followed him.

Everyone was soon sitting in the morning sun, drinking coffee and eating muffins. Carrie said, "These guys just ate me out of house and home and here they are eating again!" Her overnight guests were two couples that they had known in the valley. Both guys were motorcycle buddies, just like Dennis and Ron.

Suddenly, maybe twenty minutes into the gathering, Carrie noticed Dennis' jaw and said, "My god, Dennis, what happened to your face?" The six from next door all crowded around and looked at the deepening bruise.

Dennis Insisted it looked worse than it was. "What happened? You left our house with a whole face." You could tell Jack was upset—perhaps thinking Dennis had too much to drink before leaving and he fell or something.

"Hold it! Jack, I didn't fall on my face or anything. I was clobbered in the middle of the night by an intruder. You should have seen Ron chasing him down that hill. Ron's robe was flapping and he was pumping along like an old lady. Lost the dude, too."

I said, "How would you know Ron's robe was flapping? You were in a heap on the floor when Ron went flying out of the house."

Dennis sat there for a minute and said, "By god, you're right. I guess I heard you telling the cop or something."

I elbowed Dennis; we were back on the glider. "I did not tell the police that Ron went running with robe flapping. Did I, Donna?"

Donna said, "No one said anything about flapping robes. You must have been hallucinating, Dennis."

Everyone laughed. When the giggles had settled down, Jack asked, "Who was it? Have any clue?" We all shook our heads.

"He had his arm up shielding his face when he bulldozed me in the hallway. Dennis said he was whacked as he came out of the bathroom and the bedroom was dark. Ron chased him but couldn't tell too much. No one knows. The police checked the area where a vehicle had been parked at the edge of Mclean. The unique tire pattern indicates it was a vehicle with dual rear wheels. That's the most we know about our night visitor. We didn't get back to bed until after 4am."

"And," Dennis continued, "it's all my fault because I had been asked to lock the door when I came home and I forgot."

Carrie and Jack were whispering between themselves. "What's up?" Dennis asked them. "Do you have an idea who it was? Or, better yet, why?"

Carrie said, "We do know someone with a dual wheeled vehicle but I can't imagine it was him. What do the police say?"

The four of us tried talking at once and the other six got the impression that the police didn't say anything of great importance. Which is true.

Finally Jack said, "Well, let's worry about this later. We have important dates to make. He pulled a rolled up wall calendar out of his jacket and laid it on the table. I moved the coffee service to one of the tables by the glider.

"Carrie, Donna, gals, do you want to come in and let these guys get their calendars scheduled?" I brought Ron and Donna's breakfast dishes in. "Carrie, go ahead into the living room. I want to start the dishwasher. See if anyone wants more coffee; I'll make another pot."

The five of us settled in the living room and had a pleasant hour or so of girl talk. Carrie and I were anxious for news of the valley and Carrie's California friend had a lot of updates for her. We talked for quite a while. I asked if any of them had ever gone to Dumont Dunes with their husbands. Carrie said she had gone once with Jack, before they were married. She told us the story of the wildest weekend she had ever experienced before marrying Jack. I guess there have been a few since marrying him. We were practically rolling on the floor by the time she finished. Her last lines of the story made us laugh even harder. "I thought he was dead and all the time I was running to the sandrail I was wondering what in the world am I going to tell his mother. I hadn't met her yet."

The five guys came in about then and Jack asked, "What is so funny?" We laughed harder and pointed at him.

He turned to his buddies and said, "Women!" We laughed even harder. "Okay, who wants a tour of Payson? We have a couple cars or we can walk around town. Carrie works about a mile from here to the north—my job is even closer. We have a few notable spots—McDonald's and a KFC. Anything else, Carrie?"

In the end, everyone decided we should take two cars and check out the golf course, Pioneer Cemetery, the post office, library, Grizzly Adam's cabin, all the hot spots. Then we'll meet at the Winchester Saloon for a drink mid-afternoon. Carrie reminded us that we have a party scheduled to start at 9.

I asked Carrie how many were coming. She said, "Charles and Mary for sure; the Willards and Posts from up the Ridge; Lyle thinks he can make it. Probably 18 or 19 people, including all of us. I have the goodies pretty much under control. Just need to make the punch."

Jack drives an American Motors Javelin that is a two-door so I drove my Buick and Jack took Carrie's car. The guys were in one car, the gals in my car. We are all going to see the same places but, as it turned out, not at the same time. We met at the Winchester Saloon at 3:30pm. What a great day!

Everyone was quite impressed with the Winchester. It's a huge two-story building done in rough pine. The bar is 40 feet long. Upstairs is a banquet hall; downstairs a drinking hall. They serve all the potent potables you could wish for plus a few munchies. The most impressive part? Walking out on the front porch of the saloon and looking almost straight up at our two houses. The primary comment seemed to be "Wow! Straight up!"

Mclean comes north off the main highway by the turnoff to the Indian Reservation. It meets Main Street and follows Main Street for a block or so and then turns north right at the Winchester. Our two houses are the first two on the south side of Summit Ridge. There are two little east-west streets between Main and Summit but because of the angle from the Winchester, you can't see them well, if at all.

Nearly everyone got something to eat at the saloon. Everyone had something to drink. It was close to 6pm when we decided to head home. We girls left first. Most of us were ready for a short nap. All that fresh air—it was around 55 degrees—makes for a tired feeling when you finally slow down. Donna went with Carrie and the other two gals; Eve and Nan I think. I can be so bad about names and I don't think I was introduced to them. They're married to Roger and Bill—I think. Carrie invited me to come up to her house as well but I figured she should have time alone with her old friends. They talked about places, people and things that I didn't know this afternoon Carrie seemed to think she had to explain them to me and that made me feel a bit awkward.

Since I am hosting New Year's Day I had a lot of things to get together anyhow so welcomed the time. I was putting veggies and cheese in the fridge when Dennis came to the door. "Eleanor, we stopped at some place Jack knows and picked up something to eat. Want to come up? Smells good!"

I thought it would be churlish of me to refuse so said, "Sure, let me finish putting this food away." He waited for me. I took a coat sweater off a hook behind the door. I locked the back and front doors and followed him up the walkway.

"How long have you lived in Payson, Eleanor?" Dennis was a very friendly guy. I told him, briefly, how and when I came to be in Payson. "Wow! Then you aren't an old timer either." I admitted I wasn't. "Well, we all hated to see Jack and Carrie move to Arizona. And then when they moved up here, I thought the distance alone might be too much for even long weekends. But it's not bad. And, we can still meet in Dumont Dunes or wherever—we've been friends for a long time. Jack can meet Roger and Bill at the bottom of this mountain—" He stopped mid-sentence. "I didn't mean to bore you with details. We're just all anxious to go riding again with Jack. He's crazy, you know."

I nodded. "Oh, yes, I know."

The guys had evidently gone to Pedro Wong's and picked up egg rolls and mini burritos and some salsa and chips. We sat on the Bayh's deck and just talked. Finally Carrie said, "We should really get ready for a party. Neighbors and friends will begin arriving soon."

Ron said, "What are we, chopped liver?" Carrie threw a cushion at him and everyone laughed. But she was right. It was getting late; the sun had already hid itself behind the mountains. It was nearly dark. I was glad for the company as I walked home. Ron and Donna followed Dennis and I. They are seriously talking buying a vacation house in Payson and staying an extra day to do some house hunting. Dennis is leaving late tomorrow afternoon to go back to California.

The party was in full swing by 10. All the neighbors who were wintering in Payson on Summit Ridge had come. I was surprised that most of them didn't know one another. We three houses on the west end of the road were the only ones that knew anyone else on the street.

Carrie put a coat tree in the corner of the family room by the door to the deck. She figured that someone would be in and out all evening. It was a bit nippy but not freezing on the deck. There was no wind so it was invigorating to catch a breath of air on the deck now and then.

Jack had the television in the family room on and had celebrated the coming of the New Year in every time zone around the world, I think. Chicago had just set off fireworks when Fletcher came in the front door. Jack greeted him; offered him a drink; showed him the buffet and then said, "If you really want to go bike riding with us sometime, come into the family room and I'll show you the planned dates. We'll all meet in Baker and caravan to Dumont Dunes."

I slipped my coat off the rack and went out on the deck. A couple neighbors were there and we got into a discussion of how long everyone has lived in Payson. It is interesting. Jim and Polly have had the house on Summit Ridge for 16 years but only became year round residents two years ago. We talked back yards, retaining walls, apple trees and I told them about our supper club. "It's my turn to host next—though there's no set date. But if you'd like to come, I'll let you know when a date is set."

They thought that would be a lot of fun. Polly said, "I really need to go inside. Do you want me to bring anything back?" Jim asked for some of the crab dip and she promised she'd return with it—in a few minutes.

Jim and I made small talk for the few minutes Polly was gone. When she came out with the crab dip and crackers, Fletcher held the door for her. And, of course, he came out too.

"So, this is where you've been hiding." He tried to put his arm around me and I turned away. "Come on, Eleanor. It's New Year's Eve. Be a little friendly."

"Of course, Fletcher. Jim and Polly, do you know Fletcher Ellison? He's an attorney in the Swiss Village." I thought to myself—"That's being friendly, isn't it?"

Jim shook Fletcher's hand. "Do you specialize in any particular type of law, Mr. Elllison?"

Fletcher, being the person he is, couldn't walk away from an interested person and in a matter of seconds was engrossed in telling Jim about his practice which led to a half dozen lawyer jokes which led to other jokes. As Jim and Polly were being entertained, I went into the house, hung up my coat and looked for the punch bowl. Carrie makes an unusual juice punch and then spikes it. Very tasty.

Jack saw me at the buffet table and called to me, "It's finally almost midnight in our time zone." I took a plate of goodies and a cup of punch and went into the family room.

"So, is Fletcher actually going riding with you guys?" Personally, I find it a bit hard to envision him on a motorcycle. "He doesn't own a bike, does he?"

"I'm going to loan him one of my little bikes. He'd kill himself on the bikes we ride." Jack helped himself to my plate.

"Little bike? Will he go for that?"

"Come on, Eleanor. You know what I mean. He can ride my CanAm 125. It's got power but not as much as the dirt bikes." Jack got up and went for more food. He brought me some more punch. "I'm not sure he can handle that but he sure wants to go to Baker."

Jack went into the living room where there was a raging game of Scrabble going on at one end of the room and a more raucous game of Uno at the other. "Listen up, you all. It's five minutes of midnight. Ron, got your lighter? Come on everybody—out on the deck. Hurry, hurry, we can't be late."

Everyone grabbed a coat off the rack and went out on the deck. Carrie hung back and whispered to me. "You are not going to believe this." I put my coat on wondering what next.

As the television announced midnight, Ron was at one end of the deck and Jack at the other. They both flicked their lighters and I watched as the flames ran down cords on either side of the hill behind the house. Fireworks! Jack and Ron had gone out sometime this afternoon and laid down fireworks that could be lit from the deck. It was quite amazing! We didn't have a crystal ball dropping down a tower or confetti or a big band we had fireworks! I am sure they were visible from all of Old Town, the golf course and all the houses beyond.

When the last ember was out we all went back into the house. Fletcher sidled up to me and whispered, "Whatever happened to kissing your girl at midnight?"

I whispered back, "It's still a tradition. All you need is your own girl." I went back to the couch where I had left my punch.

Fletcher found Jack and said, "Since Eleanor won't kiss me for the New Year, I am going to take my hat and go home. But I'll mark my calendar for the last weekend in January to go bike riding with you guys." He went around and shook hands, told Jim and Polly to make an appointment next week for their wills, and left.

Maybe 1981 will be a better year. Maybe.

Jack, Carrie and their houseguests didn't get to my house until after 10 New Year's Day. Dennis and I made cinnamon rolls and hot chocolate and were watching the Rose Parade from Pasadena when they came in. I started to get up and Dennis said, "Stay where you are. I know where everything is." He went to the kitchen and filled a tray with breakfast stuff and set it on the table in front of the couch. Everyone helped himself and watched the rest of the parade and then the rerun. Just as the parade rerun was starting, Ron and Donna got up.

Soon everyone was reliving the times they had gone to the Rose Parade in person. Some slept overnight on the parade route while others walked three miles to avoid traffic. That reminded Carrie of the year they were married—Jack had driven his car along the parade route just before midnight. "So what's so special about that?" I'm not sure who asked.

"Well," said Carrie. "He drove it backwards. The police stopped him because they said the law required a white light on the front of a vehicle. And if he was driving backwards then the back was the front. I'm not sure exactly how they put it. I was laughing too hard. Fortunately, we hadn't been drinking so they couldn't get us for DUI. And when Jack showed them he'd taken one taillight lens off and had a white light in the back, they just threw up their hands and walked away. Then one officer came back and suggested it would be a lot less confusing for other motorists if he didn't drive backwards."

We were all roaring with laughter by the time she finished. I could tell Jack thought it was pretty special that she had told the story. The guys had to talk about that and it got so noisy that we took our cups out to the deck. "Guys." We said it almost simultaneously. And we laughed even more.

The day flew by and soon Dennis was saying goodbye. He wanted to get home in time for work the next morning. "Thanks for a great time, Eleanor. I'll stop by next time I'm in Payson."

I told him that sounded like a plan. We all followed him out to his jeep. He yelled at Ron, "What do you want me to tell the boss?"

Ron yelled back, "Tell him I'll be back day after tomorrow. Maybe." Dennis waved as he went down the hill. When he reached Main Street, he stopped and waved again. I think he had a good time. I know I was happy to have met him. He's the kind of guy that could be a good friend.

The next day Ron and Donna went house hunting. And they found just what they wanted on Pine, a little street that runs east of the highway just after you enter town from the south. The realtor put together the package and came into the title office. Escrow should close in four or five weeks. The owner doesn't live in Payson fulltime so it may take a little time.

That afternoon, at work, six white roses were delivered. The card read, "You should have kept tradition and kissed me on New Year's Eve. Fletcher."

Yeah, right!

Chapter Nineteen

The month seemed to hurry by. We sent the escrow owner signed papers to Jack's friend Ron and they were returned promptly. The little house on Pine would need some paint before summer and Jack figured he'd try to set up a "paint party" with Ron at the next bike ride. Jack was getting his trailer and bikes ready to go down Highway 87 to Mesa. There he'd hook up with his friends and they'd meet Ron and Dennis in Baker. Jack offered to pick up Fletcher at home but Fletcher suggested they meet at his office.

Carrie and I planned dinner out that evening. She said she'd found a few things while filing that seem suspicious to her. She wants to discuss them with me and see what I think. Everything that is bothering her is in Fletcher's personal files.

After dinner she pulled a file folder out of her bag. The Quit Claim Deed he brought to the title office had been recorded and returned to him. He just got around to giving it to her to file a week ago. And his divorce papers—he'd pulled them to prove to her he was single. Well, those and a couple of other documents don't look right to her. She made copies of the signatures and notary—she said, "I'm not an expert but look at this. The notary signatures on the deed and divorce paper don't look like the signatures on the wills that Mary Ellen notarized before she left. And the principle signature on both documents look pretty much alike. But one is supposed to be his wife's and one his brother's.

"And, on top of that, Fletcher had me check the calendar to be sure he didn't owe Mary Ellen any more vacation pay. The days both these documents were notarized, Mary Ellen was not in the office." Carrie ordered a second drink.

"Where does his brother live?" I couldn't remember seeing an address on the deed when I sent it for recording.

"That's another problem. His brother lives in Texas." Carrie took a large drink of her bourbon.

"Texas? That can't be. When he brought the deed into the office, he said it hadn't been ready when he left that morning for the County Seat. If his brother lives in Texas and Mary Ellen was off, how did this get signed and notarized while he was gone?" I could see her problem. She works for a crook and this appears to be proof.

"If you're sure that's what he said, I am going to ask him when his brother was last in Payson." Carrie looked like she had something figured out. "He won't know what you told me and won't have any reason to lie. I've filed all this stuff so he shouldn't connect the dots."

Twice over that weekend, Carrie came over to suggest maybe she should check other documents in his personal file. I warned her. "Be very careful, Carrie. He is a dangerous man. Be very careful."

Late Sunday evening Jack pulled into their driveway. He had already dropped Fletcher off at his office. I guess because my lights were still on he thought it okay to call. "Eleanor, I know it's late but can you come up for a couple minutes? I'll explain when you get here."

"Sure, I'll put on some shoes and be right over." Jack sounded more wary than upset. I wonder what now??

"Care for a drink?" Jack was pouring himself a rather stiff one.

I shook my head. "Thanks. I've had my quota for the day." Actually, taking into consideration dinner Friday evening and Carrie's drop ins on Saturday and Sunday, I'd had my month's quota already.

"What's up?" I hung my coat and sat on the couch.

"This weekend was the damndest thing. I need to bounce it off both of you." He put his arm around Carrie. "Fletcher is some far out dude."

Carrie hadn't told him yet about the suspicious signatures so this new revelation, what ever it was going to be, might push her out of a job. "Why? What happened?" We asked him in unison.

"Well, I doubt that he'll ever go with us again although we all reminded him when we plan to go next. The man can't stay on a bike. Even my little CanAm—he dropped it at least a dozen times. He's probably bruised pretty badly. The bike is really scratched up. Dennis and Ron kept calling him 'Fall down Fletcher'. It wasn't pretty.

"I went up to the office to pick him up and he asked if we were going through Baker proper. I told him yes. He says, can we stop at my great-aunt's and drop off the Christmas presents I never got sent to her. How could I tell him no. I said sure if you don't dawdle too much. It's going to be late. Are you sure she'll be up? And he said not to worry.

"So, we get into Baker and he directs us into this little residential district. There was a porch light on and he ran up to the door with 3 or 4 gifts in his arms. He wasted no time. But a guy came to the door, not an old lady. He said it was his second cousin or something. I don't remember. Anyhow, we connected with everybody else back on the highway and went on to Dumont Dunes. Probably because of the time of year, there weren't a whole lot of people and we found a place against some small dunes to pitch our tents.

"The next morning we had to rouse him out of his sleeping bag. He didn't want to get up so early, I guess, but that's neither here nor there. We rode out to the amphitheater dune. Roger had brought his sand rail and Bill brought an old dune buggy with a roll bar cage he added and we all had bikes.

"I showed Fletcher how to start the bike. Twenty feet and he was on the ground. He doesn't take ribbing too well and it didn't improve his riding. That man is a disaster.

"But what bothers me more than his lack of coordination was the package drop off. There's something strange about that. Any ideas if I'm off base with thinking there's some illegal going on here?"

Carrie looked at me and I looked at her. "What? What?" Jack asked. "What's going on?"

So Carrie told him what she thinks she's found in Fletcher's files. We all agree something more is afoot. Jack wants her to quit, immediately. I said, "Jack, if she does, Fletcher will think you know something. And you don't—you just suspect something."

He agreed and told Carrie to be sure to be very careful in the office. "Don't take chances; keep your notary stuff under lock and key and be careful." I seconded the motion.

Jack walked me back to the house. Because sound carries and I never know where Fletcher might be hiding, we talked about Dumont Dunes and how my husband and I used to go there . . . anything except what was on our minds. And he told me that Ron and his wife would be up the week before Easter to do some painting at the Pine Street house. He came in with me and noticed my answering machine was flashing.

I said, "That's strange. I've only been gone a few minutes. Who would call so late?"

Jack said, "Law of averages—the minute you walk out the phone rings."

I punched the button. Nothing. There were 5 empty calls.

Jack asked, "Who do you suppose?"

"Fletcher," I replied. "He's done it before." Just then the phone rang. I jumped as I was right on top of the phone. Then I answered it. "Hello." No one was there. I hung up.

Jack said, "He's really crazy, isn't he?"

"Jack, don't ever tell him that or he'll pull out his release papers from the State of Texas Mental Health Department. He has proof he's sane." Jack just looked at me and began whooping.

"You're joking!"

"No, I'm not." I related the Christmas dinner story from Diamond Point. Jack shook his head.

"I think I'll head home on that note. Lock your doors, Eleanor. Sleep well." I watched him go up the ridge to his house before closing and locking the door. I checked all the other doors, and windows, before turning out the lights and going to bed.

Over the next few weeks, Carrie found a number of definitely suspicious notary work and land transfer signatures. She also found a property settlement between Fletcher and his wife that had not been signed. She returned it to the place she found it. The settlement gave him everything but an old beat up car that Mrs. Ellison drives. That meant the property she had when she married him, the house she lives in and has owned for years and a large Treasury bond are all going to be his if the settlement is signed.

We are pretty sure she is unaware that she is supposedly divorced when we found out Fletcher still lives with her. Jack joked with me that the reason Fletcher was so anxious to get on my good side was so he could move out of his wife's house. I said I felt more like he wanted my property too.

Carrie brought photocopies of anything suspicious including a couple of wills that made Fletcher all but sole beneficiary. I told her I didn't think some of the will work was even legal. She doesn't know as she's never done wills before working for Fletcher. But she's made copies of those too.

Then she panicked about keeping the stuff at her house. I now have a fat little file in my craft room tabbed "New/different knitting patterns". The file is stuck in with a bunch of other folders regarding yarns, patterns, stuff like that. I don't know what she plans to do with it but I'll keep it for her.

Valentine's Day brought me five exquisite white roses in a red heart vase. The card read, "Be my Valentine. Have dinner with me Friday. Fletcher" Duane asked if I am ever going to relent and date Fletcher. I told him I didn't think so.

Chapter Twenty

About a month after Valentine's Day Jack was scheduled to meet his friends again to go biking. He called Fletcher at work one afternoon and asked if he was going to be able to go. Fletcher said he didn't think so. But, if not, could Jack drop another package off at his great-aunt's house? Jack almost stammered and then said he could.

Carrie didn't want Jack to take the packages but Jack said he couldn't figure a way to refuse without Fletcher getting suspicious. So the day before Jack was going, Fletcher brought 3 rather large packages to Jack. They were wrapped in very gaudy paper—though it didn't seem like birthday wrap or any particular occasion—just really bright paper with ribbons wrapped around it like a kid may have wrapped it.

When Jack saw the packages he said they were 'tamper proof' wrapped. No way could Jack unwrap the packages and rewrap them without destroying paper or ribbon. That made him even more suspicious.

When he and his friends got to the house in Baker, a woman answered the door. All three guys thought it was a young woman trying to look old.

Late that Sunday evening Fletcher called Jack to see if his "aunt" had been at home. Or was his second cousin there? Jack told him that some woman answered the door and was just delighted that dear, dear Fletcher had sent her gifts. Fletcher said something like 'that sounds like Aunt Abby."

Jack was not convinced.

Meanwhile my folder of patterns was growing. One Saturday Carrie came over and we were sitting on the deck watching the first hummingbirds arrive. I put up three feeders as Charles, across the street, says he thinks we are on a hummingbird migration route. But my house gets more birds than his because mine is on a southern facing hillside. There were several green-throated hummingbirds that morning.

Carrie said that she has been keeping track of Fletcher's out of office time. About every six weeks or so, he gets a telephone call from a man who calls himself Mr. Drago. "It's strange," Carrie told me. "This man calls and I pass the call to Fletcher. He gets up and closes his office door—after he has made sure I am no longer on the line. I think he believes he's being subtle but I have actually seen him check on me before he closes the door."

"What do you suppose that's all about?" I poured some more tea for us both.

"I'm not sure. But yesterday when Mr. Drago called I passed the call and then got up and went to the filing cabinets. Fletcher stuck his head out of his office but I was very involved in filing and he said nothing. He closed his door and took the call. But the door wasn't closed all the way and from where I was standing I could see the safe in his office. While he was talking to Mr. Drago, he opened the safe and took out a small folded paper. It looked something like a map when he opened it. Then he realized the door wasn't completely closed and he got up and shut it firmly. Of course, I was still filing.

But before he closed the door, I heard him say 'the 29th, sure that's a good day. So I've made a small mark on my desk calendar on the 29th to remind me to keep track of him that day."

I guess I am dense. I just don't understand what Carrie is trying to do.

"What is that going to prove?" I asked her.

"Well, I am pretty sure that every time this man has called, Fletcher was late to the office a day or two later. I think he's picking up something—or something. I don't know. I'm grasping at straws, I guess."

We sat and watched the birds for a while in silence. Then Carrie said, "I am just sure he's into something illegal."

"Like what?" Personally I already think he's into something illegal—like stealing property and phony divorces and stuff.

"Maybe drugs. Isn't it convenient that he has a great-aunt right in Baker where Jack passes through periodically?" She poured the tea.

"Oh, lord, Carrie, I hope you're wrong. Jack, Roger and Bill could all be in trouble if they're transporting drugs across state lines. Well, transporting drugs, period." Just then I thought I heard someone or something by the garage. Someone was definitely walking on the gravel. I got up to look over the end of the deck. There was Fletcher—trying to tiptoe over the gravel—coming up the path to the stairs.

"Well, Fletcher Ellison, what brings you here?" I tried to be bright and cheery in voice if not attitude. I walked down the porch to meet him.

"I wanted to see Carrie and since no one is home at her house, I thought she might be here. So I walked down." By this time, Carrie was on her feet and right behind me.

She whispered to me, "How long has he been there?"

"I think he was just coming down." I whispered back. Fletcher was at the bottom of the steps to my deck. Carrie walked a few feet toward him.

"Come on up. What do you need, Boss?"

"Actually, I need the key to the bottom drawer of your desk." Fletcher came onto the deck.

Carrie got a puzzled look on her face. "What in the world for? I keep my personal junk in there. Hand lotion, mouthwash, tissues, cold remedies."

His face got quite red. "Isn't the first aid kit there?"

"Oh, no, the first aid kit is in the bathroom behind your office. Remember, you said that it would be handiest there because you know first aid?" Carrie went back to the table and sat down. "If you need some first aid, maybe Eleanor or I can help you."

"No, no. I just bought some gauze and tape and stuff to put into it. I'm afraid if I leave it in the truck until Monday, I'll forget it." The blush had receded but he still seemed hesitant.

Carrie said, "Well, if you want to leave it with me, I'll be sure to get it into the first aid kit Monday."

"No, that's okay. Just remind me Monday when I come in to go back to the truck and get the bag from the drugstore." He turned and headed back toward the steps.

"Okay, I'll do that." Carrie was very cheery now, for real. "See you Monday. Have a good weekend."

I went inside and watched him go up my driveway to Carrie's house. Sure enough—his pickup was parked in front of her house. A few minutes later we saw him go down Mclean and turn onto Main Street. However, he didn't head south out of town as if he was going home.

"What do you suppose that was all about?" I asked Carrie as we brought the teapot and cups inside.

"My notary stuff is locked in that bottom drawer along with my hand lotion and cold remedies. I am quite sure he'll pick the lock. But I took the seal out of the embosser so it won't be of any use to him—if he notices. And, he won't dare mention it. If he does, I'll tell him that I got something stuck in the seal so I brought it home to try and clean it." Carrie was definitely being careful.

When she went into the office Monday, she was sure that the drawer had been opened. She had set little markers, invisible unless you knew what they were. She replaced the seal in her notary embosser and relocked the drawer. Just after 9, Fletcher came in with a bag of first aid supplies. He hadn't removed the sales register tape. It was dated Saturday, about an hour after he had been to my house looking for Carrie. She's sure he is unaware that the pharmacy put in a new cash register that dates and times every transaction.

"Fletcher, do you want reimbursement from petty cash?" Carrie told me she asked him so innocently. "Is that why you left the receipt in the bag?" He told her yes, that was the general idea. Something about gauze being so damned expensive anymore. She counted out $8.12 and put it on his desk and marked the receipt paid—right across the date and time—and put it into the petty cash box.

The morning of the 29th, Fletcher was nearly two hours late coming in to the office. After work, Carrie came down to my house to return a cake mold. She said, "He was late. And, he had on dress slacks not overalls like usual. I am sure he met someone."

That weekend was another bike tour. But this time, Fletcher called Jack to see if he was still going to meet the guys. Jack told him he was. And, again, Fletcher asked if Jack would deliver another package to Aunt Abby. I was at Jack and Carrie's when the call came. While I don't know Jack well, I do know that he normally doesn't blanche while talking on the phone. After he hung up, he told us that he had agreed to take another package to Baker.

Carrie said, "Jack, isn't there some way you can get out of it? I am so sure he's into something very, very illegal. I don't want you to go to jail for him."

Jack just shook his head. "I don't know what to do. Next week I am going down to the valley for that new mechanic's test. I am going to talk to an attorney Bill knows. We can't prove anything against Fletcher. And the law doesn't act on hunches." We all shook our heads in unison and that got Jack laughing. "God, we three are a real mess. Pour me another drink Carrie."

Chapter Twenty-One

On the way to Baker that weekend, a tire blew on the trailer. Jack didn't have a spare so the three guys had to fix the tire on the side of I-10. Just before they put the tire back on, an Arizona State Patrol car stopped. The officer asked if they needed help and the guys joked about his timing. He asked where they were headed and they told him Dumont Dunes. Then he asked where they were coming from. Jack said he was from Payson and Bill and Roger said Mesa.

The officer looked into the car and asked what was in the packages on the back floor. Jack said he was scared spitless but managed to say that his wife's boss had asked him to deliver some gifts to an aunt in Baker. The officer asked if he knew what was in the packages. Jack had said something to the effect that he hadn't even thought about it—they were personal gifts.

Then the officer wanted to know what the address was where the gifts were to be delivered. Jack said he pulled the address from his wallet and read it to the officer. They finished putting the lug nuts on the wheel and the officer told them to have a safe trip.

"Honest to god, Eleanor." Jack was shaking while talking to me. "I thought sure that cop was going to open a package and I'd be in jail. I am sure Carrie's right. Fletcher is definitely into something illegal and I think he's got me involved too. Some friend."

"And on top of it, he called me Sunday night and asked why I was so late getting into Baker."

"What?" I couldn't imagine how he'd know when Jack got to Baker.

"He said that his aunt had called him and told him that I had been quite a bit later than she expected and she had to wait up for me. I told him we'd had a flat on the trailer and no spare. It took a while to repair the tire in the middle of the damn desert." Jack was upset with Fletcher for sure. I have never seen him so agitated. He was pacing up and down the deck waving his glass around. "I am not going to take any more packages for him. And that's final."

Dinner was a subdued affair that evening. Jack was ticked by Fletcher's phone call. He kept muttering about it throughout the meal. By the time I left for home at 8 he had finally calmed down. But he was adamant about no more gifts to Baker for Fletcher.

The week before Easter Ron, Donna and a couple of their friends called Jack to say they were in Payson and going to get some lunch before going to the house. Did he and Carrie want to join them?

"You're going to feed us lunch so we'll help you clean and paint, huh?" He listened for Ron's reply and hung up laughing. "Okay, sweets, ready to put on your paint duds?" He took Carrie by the hand and pulled her off the bench.

I said, "Well, have a good time. How many of you will there be? I could bring something over late afternoon to drink, if you like." Jack thought that would be really nice. I had an ulterior motive. I wanted to see Dennis again. I had felt so comfortable around him at New Years.

About 3 the phone rang. It was Jack. The telephone had just been installed at Ron's and they wanted to try it out. "How's the painting going?" I thought I'd be polite and ask.

"Hey, you should be here. Dennis is telling everybody what a great hostess you are and that you really know how to cook."

I blushed, glad that this was a phone call. "I wasn't invited to help so I am just here baking cookies."

"Are you planning on bringing some over to us?" Jack was teasing, I think.

"Of course, I am. I've made some lemonade and tea and will be there as soon as the last batch of cookies are off the sheets."

Jack yelled to the group in the house, "Want Eleanor to bring some lemonade and stuff?" The cheers were loud so I guess so. "Come ahead. You know where we are, right? Just look off your deck. Can you see that little street right north of the pass? That's Pine. It's steep but passable."

"I know where Pine is, Silly. I'll be there pretty soon. Should I bring my paintbrush or something?"

"Sure, if you're good at moldings and window frames."

"They are my specialties. I'll be there soon." I was glad that I hadn't gone earlier. This way I was doubly welcome—cookies and a paintbrush.

I am embarrassed to say that I took extra care putting my hair up and put on a decent shirt over my jeans. If Dennis was talking about me as Jack said perhaps he was interested in me. I was humming as I loaded things into the car.

The afternoon went quickly. I got all the moldings done in the rooms they had finished as well as all the windows. About 8 Dennis asked for a time out and said he didn't know about anyone else but he was hungry. We were all more or less paint spattered and Jack asked me, "Do you think they'll let us in at Mario's?"

I thought they would. We all crammed into two cars and caravanned to the restaurant—which was just across the highway from Pine Street. So it was definitely close enough. No one at Mario's seemed to think we were out of line in our paint clothes and we were seated at a large table in the middle of the room. It was a great meal. The beer and red wine flowed freely. Ron said he thought we should just resume our labors tomorrow. Everyone was willing to drink to that. We didn't leave Mario's until nearly 11.

Dennis and I had sat together and enjoyed good conversation. I am actually looking forward to tomorrow.

Chapter Twenty-Two

Spring quickly moved into early summer. The azaleas were more beautiful this year than last. Our back yards were seas of white and pink. Duane gave me a raise at the end of May. I was quite pleased with it. He said he'd like to have given me a promotion or a title as well but the office is just too small. I told him I was pleased with the raise. He invited me to a Memorial Day picnic at his house. "Bring your neighbors too. We'll bar-b-que something."

Jack and Carrie thought it would be a lot of fun. They had met Duane when they bought the house but hadn't seen him since. So, on Memorial Day, the three of us drove to Duane's. We were in the middle of eating when Fletcher pulled into the yard. I looked at Carrie and she looked at me. We both looked at Duane. He rolled his eyes and said, "I mentioned to Fletcher that we might bar-b-que today. I don't remember inviting him though."

He went to the truck and shook Fletcher's hand and invited him to the table. Fletcher took over the party with his jokes. He asked Duane if he had any gin—he could sure use a good martini. He talked non-stop for a long while until Jack couldn't take it anymore. He said to Duane, "We really have to leave. Thanks so much for inviting us. We'll have to have you over for dinner some time. Carrie's a great cook."

Duane walked us to the car. "I am sorry. Honestly, I didn't invite him. He asked what we were doing for the holiday. I should never have told him I was bar-b-queing. Thanks for coming. And again, I am sorry."

It was a quiet ride home.

The following Saturday the lady who owns the local thrift shop called me and said that someone had just brought in a lot of knitting things. Did I want to come look? I called Carrie and we went to the shop.

While I was looking over the knitting needles, Carrie was checking out the blue jeans. "Hey, Eleanor, what do you think of these?" She had tried on a pair.

"Other than the fact that they're about 7 inches too long, they're great."

"I can go retro and roll up the cuffs like in the 50s." Carrie turned around in front of the mirror. "They really fit well. And, they're only a dollar."

Well, who could argue with logic like that? "Buy them." I told her. She did. She rolled up the cuffs and wore them home.

Jack laughed at her but agreed the jeans fit very well. Carrie is a petite girl and looks really great in blue jeans.

Fletcher had a call from Mr. Drago two days before the next bike ride date. He again asked Jack to take some packages to Baker. Jack said he told him that since Aunt Abby was so ticked because he was late last time, he didn't think he wanted to see her again.

Fletcher was livid. His aunt is a weak-minded old lady. She likes the goodies he sends but doesn't understand things like flat tires and time and such. Jack wavered for just a moment and Fletcher said he'd bring the packages over after work the day Jack was leaving. Jack reminded him that he would be leaving by 4pm as he had to meet Bill and Roger in Mesa by 5:30 or so.

Fletcher brought four packages this time; wrapped in plain brown paper. He told Jack he was ticked at Aunt Abby and wasn't going to waste wrapping paper on her. The packages were tied with white strings.

When Jack got to Mesa, he called a number the attorney had given him. Then he met his two friends and they took off for Baker.

Ten miles past Tonapah they were pulled over by the Arizona State Police. The officer shook Jack's hand and assured him that he had done the right thing. Jack said he wasn't even sure if his suspicions were right but he had to find out.

The officer took one of the packages back to the patrol car. Fifteen minutes later he returned it. It looked just as it looked when he took it. "Are these packages being delivered to the same address in Baker as the last?' Jack said that they were. The officer told him that he had been right—he was delivering drugs, not gifts, to Baker. Jack was to deliver the packages as usual and go on to Dumont Dunes.

Fletcher called Jack Sunday evening. I was there getting the whole story when he called. He wanted to know if Jack had run into any trouble on the way. Jack told him no. No flats or anything this trip. He had delivered the packages as promised before the old lady's bedtime. Fletcher pushed for more information. Jack said, "Fletcher, I dropped the packages off and went on to meet my friends. There's nothing more I can tell you. What's your problem, man? Maybe you better get someone else to run your errands for you." He slammed down the phone and paced around the living room.

Carrie asked him, "What else did the officer say?"

"Nothing. Just deliver and go on." Jack went out to the kitchen and was looking through the contents of the fridge. He saw some fried chicken in a container and pulled it out. Picking up a napkin from the counter, he came back into the living room. "He didn't say anything else—except that I was delivering drugs and to do it and go riding."

The attorney Jack had talked with had made contact with the DEA and they seemed anxious to get to the guy shipping the stuff to Baker. They didn't want Jack or his buddies. Jack had been plenty nervous about calling when he got to Mesa that Friday but, so far, everything seems okay. He's not in jail anyhow. But neither is Fletcher.

That's why Fletcher's call didn't make sense. He wasn't delayed. He'd delivered all four packages. "That boss of yours is going to be the death of me, Carrie." Jack was talking with his mouth full.

The next day when Carrie got to the office, Fletcher was already there. This was most unusual. He was on the phone when she came in but hung up almost immediately. That was unusual too.

Fletcher was sullen most of the day. He answered questions in grunts if at all. He cancelled two appointments toward the end of the day. He told Carrie if anyone was looking for him he'd be at the Chalet. She took messages and made excuses for the rest of the day.

Spring was fading into summer. Carrie and I thought things would ease off as the guys don't go riding in the desert much after June. Too hot. Fletcher would have to find some other way to move his goods.

Then Jack was served with a subpoena to testify against a list of people he had never heard of. He called the court trying to find out what it was all about and the clerk told him to appear as ordered. She didn't know anything else. Like an idiot, his term not mine, Jack asked Fletcher if a person had to respond to a subpoena if he didn't know who the people were that were named as defendants.

Fletcher wanted to know what he was talking about and Jack showed him the subpoena. Fletcher turned very pale when he read it. Jack told Carrie and I later that he thought Fletcher was going to pass out. He told Jack that he would have to appear as ordered. This was a federal subpoena for testimony in a federal court.

Then Jack got a notice that his appearance was being continued. Carrie explained to us that meant it was being delayed. Instead of early July, he had to appear in October. We thought that was a long delay and wondered why. But since none of us knew who the defendants were, we had no clue what was going on. Finally Jack got the brilliant idea to call the attorney he had talked to in Mesa. The people listed were the people the feds had arrested in Baker with four parcels of drugs wrapped in brown paper in May.

Jack moaned and groaned. "How could I have been so stupid to show this to Fletcher? Good god, what an idiot I am!"

Meanwhile, Fletcher hadn't said anything to Carrie about anything other than what was happening in the office. They both acted as though they didn't know what was going on outside. Carrie was still gathering bits and pieces of material that proved, at least to her, that Fletcher was a grade A crook. My file was growing fatter almost daily.

The summer flew by and soon August with its vivid sunsets was in Payson. Fletcher had seemingly forgotten me—and I didn't mind a bit.

Ron and Donna spent their two weeks vacation at the little house on Pine toward the end of August. Jack and Carrie spent a lot of time there. Dennis came up for a weekend and he spent as much time at my house as he did at Jack's or Ron's. We took some good-natured ribbing from his friends. We seem to have a lot in common. Dennis had planned to come for Labor Day but his sister was moving that weekend and he had promised her months before that 'whenever you're ready, I'll be there.'

September arrived with a lightning storm that was utterly spectacular. No rain; just lightning. We sat on my deck and watched the zigzags of light for nearly an hour. Jack said he'd never seen anything like that in his life.

There were a series of Labor Day activities around town. A dance at the Elks Lodge, a bar-b-que at the Moose Lodge and several small parties. Charles and Mary invited the neighborhood to an afternoon potluck picnic and the three of us decided it'd be far more fun there than anywhere else. "And besides," Jack said, "If I drink too much I can crawl home." What a character.

Chapter Twenty-Three

The Friday before Labor Day the florist delivered four white roses to me at the office. I had been wrong. Fletcher hadn't forgotten me. He was asking me to go to the Moose Lodge with him late Labor Day and maybe swing by the Elks later for a dance or two. The card indicated he'd call me at work at 4. Good grief! What is it going to take to make him realize I'm not going out with him. Period. The roses were in a cute little vase shaped like a teddy bear. I put it on the receptionist desk. Cyndi was thrilled. Darrin never sent her flowers.

When he called at 4, I told Fletcher I had already made plans for the entire holiday weekend. He whined. He wheedled. He did everything but stomp his feet. If he'd been in my office, he probably would have done that too.

"Damn it Eleanor, why won't you go out with me? You know I'm divorced. I'm a lonely man needing a good looking woman to befriend me."

"Mr. Ellison, I'm not ready to start dating anyone yet. I really loved my husband and his death has been very hard on me." I don't know why I thought reasoning with him would work. "I am not dating anyone. End of discussion."

"I heard you were playing footsie with some guy at Mario's a couple weeks ago. Who is he? Chopped liver?"

I protested that I don't have a clue who he is talking about. It was much later that I realized Dennis and I had gone to Mario's for dinner one evening when Ron, Donna, Carrie and Jack wanted to go to the movies. There's only one theater in town and it shows the same movie all week. I don't recall what was playing but it wasn't my idea of a good view. Dennis felt the same way. We opted out of the movie and decided Italian sounded good. We had dinner and split a carafe of chianti.

Fletcher finally hung up. By then, Duane was at my office door. "I can talk to him tonight at the lounge if you want me to, Eleanor. Maybe he'll listen to me."

"I don't think so, Duane. He's used to getting his way." I finished the file I had on my desk and handed it to him. "He's like a spoiled brat. Talking won't do any good. I'm sure."

Duane suggested I leave a few minutes early as Fletcher usually walks across to the Chalet and might deliberately time his passage for 5. I left, gladly. Duane was right. Fletcher was walking out of his office as I drove past toward home.

The weekend flew by. Labor Day was a lot of fun at Charles and Mary's. I had put my car in the garage and locked everything up tight before going to their bar-b-que. Charles has a good stereo system and late afternoon he put on some good dance music and we all danced on the patio. Most of the neighborhood was there. Twice before nightfall I was sure I had heard Fletcher's big pickup lugging up the hill onto Summit Ridge. I said nothing and didn't check. But I had the feeling he was trying to figure out where we all were. Charles' backyard is sheltered by a number of trees to the west and north. Unless you knew someone was there, you'd probably not see him.

We all left shortly after sundown. My answering machine was winking wildly. Carrie and Jack came home with me. I wanted to send some extra salad home with them. All the salad I had taken to the party was eaten but I had made extra. Jack likes my pineapple cabbage salad.

The week passed quickly. Four-day weeks seem so much shorter than they are. And then the month was gone. Ron and Donna said they'd be back at Thanksgiving.

Meanwhile, Carrie had garnered a significant amount of 'evidence' against Fletcher Ellison. She was thinking perhaps she would organize it and take it to Phoenix one day. She hadn't taken any time off since she began working for Fletcher so felt she could ask for a day. And, if all went well, she wouldn't have to worry about time off. She'd be without a job and Fletcher would be in jail.

I told her things don't go that fast in the justice system. Don't collect unemployment just yet. She laughed but maintained there was no way he wouldn't end up disbarred and in jail.

In mid-October Carrie did something really very stupid. Mr. Drago called. As usual, Fletcher closed the door to his office before taking the call. He had to be in the County Court the next morning and left the office right after he took the call. Carrie packed his briefcase with the files he needed.

When she was ready to close the office for the day, she went into his office to turn out the lights. The safe door was closed but she could see it wasn't locked. She pulled the door open using a pencil. The folded map was right on top. She took it, closed the safe door and nudged the dial with the pencil to lock it. She was sure Fletcher thought he had locked the safe before leaving. He would have no reason to be back in the safe anytime soon.

Carrie stopped at my house on her way home. She was going to give me the map to add to the folder. Then, for some reason, she left without doing so. I called her later and said I was coming up. There was a ding sound on the line just before I hung up. I guess I read too many mystery stories but the sound made me think that the telephone line was bugged.

When I got to her house, I went up the back way and knocked on the kitchen door. I told her what I had heard and what I thought. She laughed. Jack came home about then and brought us each a drink out to the deck. He was getting really nervous. He had to go to Phoenix to the federal court in a few days.

Carrie went into the house and brought out her thrift shop jeans. While she was telling Jack about the sound I heard on the line and what I thought, she was tacking the cuffs up. Jack asked, "What are you doing?"

Carrie said, "You keep making fun of me because my cuffs fall down. So I am tacking them up." As I watched, she slipped the map inside the cuff she was hemming. She saw me watching her. "I have a feeling about this. I think it will be safer tucked away." Jack glanced from Carrie to me and back to Carrie.

"Do I want to know what you're talking about?"

Carrie replied, "I don't think so." She finished sewing up the cuffs and took the jeans back inside the house.

A few days later Carrie called me to see if I wanted to go with her to Safeway. Her kid brother, Rod, and some of his cronies had been camping on the Mogollon Rim and were going to stop the next day for dinner and spend the night before going on to Mesa. She figured she should stock up on a few things as Rod was a known big eater and she figured his friends probably were too.

I said that I was up to my elbows canning some late tomatoes but thanks anyway.

Chapter Twenty-Four

About an hour after Carrie had called, Jack called me looking for Carrie. I reminded him she had gone to the store for weekend food as Rod and his friends were going to be there tomorrow.

"Oh, I guess I forgot. When did she leave anyhow?" Jack sounded very confused.

"I would say it's been an hour. I really didn't look at the clock when she called. I was canning about 20 pints of tomatoes."

Jack mumbled something and then said, "Well, I thought she'd be back by now. Are you still canning?"

"No, I have just cleaned up the kitchen and am putting stuff away."

Jack mumbled again. Then he cleared his throat and said, "I'll be down in a minute."

I don't know what's going on but evidently he started to tell me something and then remembered we think the phone is bugged. I went and turned on the front porch light. The sun sets early in mid-October. In a few minutes Jack was at the door.

"What's up?" He looked awful—kind of pasty. You know, like in the old movies when someone has seen a ghost.

He came in and closed the door behind him. "Eleanor. I just got a weird telephone call. Someone warned me it wouldn't be a good idea to go down for the grand jury next week. They said I might regret it. I'm worried about Carrie. She was just going for some steaks and beer. She should have been home by now."

"Jack, it's Friday. Sometimes Safeway is crowded just before the weekend." I have to admit that didn't convince even me. "Look, I'll drive down and see if I see her car at the market."

"She's driving the Javelin. Would you check? She always comes home the back way so go down that way. Okay?" Jack stood there nervously zipping and unzipping his windbreaker. "I just can't believe it'd take an hour even on Friday. I'm going back to the house—just in case."

He didn't say just in case what but I don't think I want to know what he's thinking right now. I slipped on my jacket and locked up the house. I left the porch light on. My car was parked in the drive and I was headed east on Summit Ridge before Jack got back to his front door.

Carrie's car was not in the market parking lot. I drove up toward her office. No sign of her. I passed by the three stores I could think of where she might stop at if Safeway was out of beer. No sign of her, or Jack's car, anywhere. I pulled to the edge of Summit in front of the Bayh house and rolled down my car window. Jack was standing on the front stoop.

"Sorry, Jack. I've checked everywhere I can think of. No sign of Carrie or the Javelin."

He walked out to the car. "Do you think I should call the police?"

"You got a telephone threat and now Carrie is missing. Darn right you should call them. And don't let them give you any of that 24 hours stuff. She's missing." He turned and went back into the house. I parked my car in my driveway again.

The telephone answering machine was blinking madly again. I was just going to erase without listening and then decided I should check. The first call was Carrie—at least, it sounded like her. But all the voice said was 'warn Jack'. It sounded sort of like she had dropped the phone or someone had taken it away from her. It was very strange. The next three calls were hang ups, as usual.

I left and went to Jack's. He waved me in as he was in a heated discussion on the telephone. Finally, I signaled for a timeout and asked if that was the police. It was. I reached for the phone and he handed it to me. I told the officer on the other end of the line about the telephone call on my answering machine. He did a quick 180 and he said a patrol car would be there in a very few minutes. It was.

We went through the usual 'what was she wearing', 'what was she driving' routine you see in the movies. I didn't know what she was wearing as I hadn't seen her after work. Jack said she had on those crazy thrift shop jeans with the tacked up cuffs, a short sleeve shirt—kind of a tailored blouse he thought, some light color and brown loafers. She was driving his 1969 Javelin. The officer knew the car and wrote the description on his report.

He told Jack that because of the threat the chief was calling in the FBI. The grand jury was a federal affair that Jack was supposed to be testifying on Tuesday.

Jack told the FBI when they showed up that he was refusing to testify on Tuesday if he had no assurance that Carrie was okay. The agent said he understood how Jack felt but not testifying wasn't going to do Carrie any good. Jack said that was tough; he wasn't going to Phoenix on Tuesday. The agent said he'd make a couple calls and see if he could get a continuance.

Jack looked at me for an explanation and I told him I thought that meant that they'd postpone it for a couple days or something. The agent said, "You know, like the continuance you asked for this summer."

Jack asked what he was talking about. He had never requested a continuance. He was really upset when they pushed the date into October. The agent was sure that a request for continuance had been made by Jack or by someone acting on his behalf.

Jack and I looked at each other and said, "Fletcher!" The agent wanted to know who that was and Jack told him—briefly.

By midnight I was really tired and hungry. I had planned to eat dinner after my canning was done. I told Jack that I was going home but asked that he keep me posted. The FBI agent said he would be there so I should go ahead; Jack wouldn't be alone.

There were two more calls on the answering machine. They had to have come in after 9pm. As usual, just empty calls.

Carrie's brother showed up around noon the next day. Jack was relieved to see him. Rod suggested his friends go on home and he'd stay with Jack and worry about getting home later. I invited them all over for lunch, including Jack. The first FBI agent had been replaced by another and he said it wasn't a good idea for Jack to leave the telephone.

So Carrie's brother and his friends and I carried lunch to Jack. We ate in their dining room. I guess I watch too many movies because I was surprised that the FBI agent joined us when invited. We rehashed the entire evening for Rod. He was livid. Who had taken his sister? He had an idea why—this grand jury thing. But who had cause to want to keep Jack from testifying? Jack and I answered as one, "Fletcher Ellison."

The FBI agent talked with his office and they informed him that they had been told that Ellison had left Payson Friday evening. Jack said, "That doesn't mean he didn't hire it done. I don't trust that guy any further than I can throw him." I seconded the thought.

Rod's friends left about 3pm and said they'd call when they got home. They'd drop Rod's car by his house. I was glad that Jack had someone other than the FBI with him and I gathered up my dishes and went home. The answering machine was silent. Damn.

Rod called his parents and told them what was happening. He also said his friends would be dropping his car off; could someone take them home?. By the end of the conversation it was agreed that his father would come up Sunday so that Rod could go to work on Monday. Carrie's father would stay with Jack as long as necessary.

Figuring it best to stay out of the way, I went to work on Monday as usual. I told Duane what had happened Friday evening. He got a very strange look on his face. "Duane, what is it? Do you know something?"

Duane got up and closed his door. There were several people in the outer office already. "Eleanor, I won't swear to it but I think I saw Fletcher driving the Javelin late Friday evening. The wife and I had gone down to Rye to look at Goodwin's new log cabin model. We ended up having supper and a few drinks so it was well after 11 when we started home. We were just getting into the car when that red and white car whizzed past us on the highway. I thought at first Jack was going down to the valley to go riding but realized he wouldn't leave so late and he didn't have the trailer. But I am sure it was a man driving."

"Duane. Would you go up to the Bayh's and talk to the FBI agent that is there? Now?" Duane looked at his daily calendar.

"I have a client coming in at 10:30. Sure, I'll go now. Should I call ahead or something?" He was putting on his suit jacket as he spoke.

"I don't think it's necessary. Carrie's Dad, Mr. Johanson, is there and the FBI agent. I am sure they aren't going anywhere. Just go." I realized I had clutched his arm as I spoke and released it and stepped back. "Sorry, I guess I am more than a bit emotional about this."

"Do you want to go home, Eleanor? I am sure we could manage if you do." He opened his office door and waited for an answer.

"No, no, I'll be okay. Just keep me posted. Okay?"

Duane returned to the office about an hour later. He gave me a thumbs up and went into his office.

Chapter Twenty-Five

When I got home the next afternoon I found that the mailman had brought bulbs I had ordered during the summer. Rather than wait until the weekend to plant them, I'll just do it now. I had turned over the earth in the area I wanted to plant weeks ago so it would not be a difficult task—just time consuming.

I got out the plant food and the trowel and was soon on my knees planting tulips and daffodils. The border would be beautiful come spring. I was watering the beds when the UPS truck pulled up in front of the Bayh's. The driver took a very small package to the door.

Carrie's Dad was out on the deck and looked like he was watching the traffic come into town. Suddenly there was a scream from inside the house. Mr. Johanson ran inside and I dropped the hose and ran too. When I got there the FBI agent was holding the opened package. Jack and his father-in-law were on the sofa holding each other and crying.

I stopped inside the door and asked, "What?" Surprisingly, the agent showed me the package.

"Don't touch it. But can you identify these items?" He held the package out toward me so I could see the contents.

I felt faint. Very faint. In the little box nestled on a layer of cotton was Carrie's silver and turquoise watch and her wedding band. I am not sure but it looked to me as if there was blood on the watch. I nodded to the agent. "That's Carrie's watch and wedding ring."

The agent laid the package on top of his briefcase. "Thank you very much, Mrs. Hutchins. I was afraid that was the case." He nodded toward Jack and Mr. Johanson. "I appreciate the confirmation."

Jack released his hold on Mr. Johanson and pulled out a handkerchief and blew his nose. The older man was dabbing at his eyes and shaking his head—he looked stunned.

Jack asked the agent, "Do you think this means she's dead? That is blood isn't it?"

The agent said, "Well, I can't be sure but it appears so to me."

"Can you get hold of the court? If she's dead, I am going to testify." Jack pocketed his handkerchief. "What's the sense of letting her die for nothing?" Carrie's Dad shook his head. Apparently he agreed.

The agent said that he would make the arrangements. Jack came to me and hugged me. "It's going to be all right, Eleanor. Somehow we'll get the bastard that's done this. No matter who he is."

Just then another agent came to the door and the two men stepped outside and spoke together quietly for a number of minutes. The newly arrived agent came in and the other man left.

Mr. Johanson got up from the sofa. "Eleanor, would you like something to drink? We were discussing dinner. Care to join us?" I followed him out to the kitchen. He was struggling to appear unruffled. I watched a tear slowly creep down his check. I wanted to hold him and cry but he was setting the standard.

"I really need to get home. I think I may have left the hose running. I am planting tulip bulbs."

Mr. Johanson chuckled. "I saw you out there and wondered what you were planting. What color are the tulips?"

I told him pink and that they were supposedly the primo tulip bulb this particular company was offering for the 1982 season. We discussed tulips for a couple minutes and I reminded him the hose was running. He grinned and said, "Take it easy, Eleanor. We'll keep you informed." I thanked him and left. Jack and the new agent were head to head talking and I waved in his general direction as I went out the door.

I had left the hose running and half the yard was very well watered.

The next afternoon when I came home Mr. Johanson came over and said that they would be driving down to the valley late this evening. The FBI didn't want anyone to know so keep it mum. I promised I would. He said, "I'm not sure they would be happy if they know I've told you. But I think you need to know."

I had finished the dinner dishes and was settling down to watch the late news when Jack came up on the back deck and knocked on the kitchen door. "The guys don't know I'm here so I had better keep this short. I am going down to testify tomorrow. They think it'll run 2 or 3 days. So I may not be back until mid-week next week. Then again, I might be back Saturday—no one knows what a Grand Jury is going to do."

I acknowledged the variables possible with a grand jury. Then he went on to say, "I have been going through some of Carrie's things today. I've packed up a couple things that I think she'd want you to have. I'll put them on the deck for you. Maybe you can get them tonight. I don't want to take chances that someone would walk off with them. But I didn't want to take the chance of falling on my ass with the box coming down." He was beginning to tear up. I kissed him on the cheek and he went back to his house.

I feel so sorry for him. There is absolutely nothing I can do for him at this point. I watched him climb my driveway to Summit and enter his kitchen.

Periodically throughout the evening I checked the Bayh house and, about 10pm, saw the black government sedan pull away followed by Carrie's car. As they passed under the streetlight I could see that Carrie's dad was driving her car. He was alone so Jack must have been in the sedan.

I decided I didn't need my flashlight and walked to the Bayh's back deck. There was a fair sized box sitting on the wicker bench. It had my name on it. Carefully, I picked my way back down the ridge to my house carrying the box. The telephone was ringing as I came in. I set the box on the coffee table and answered the telephone. No one was there. But the line sounded open. I "hello-ed" a couple of times with no response so hung up.

After locking the house, front and back, I went around and drew the drapes over the large picture windows in the living room and dining room. There was a bit of chill in the air. Late October, what did I expect? I toyed with the idea of lighting a fire in the fireplace but decided I didn't want to go out to the woodpile to bring in more wood. The few logs that were inside were more decorative than useable but wouldn't have been sufficient to make a nice fire anyhow. I turned back to the television. The 11 o'clock news program from Phoenix was coming on. The evening had certainly evaporated in a hurry.

For nearly an hour I sat and stared at the box. Do I want to go through it now? I am curious what things of Carrie's Jack would have given to me but I don't believe I can handle going through it now. I got some broad cellophane tape and crisscrossed the box top and then put it in my back bedroom closet. It's the only closet in the house with a lock on the door. George and I had wondered over that when we bought the house but never bothered to make any changes. We had found a little hidey-hole that you would never know was there unless you were looking for it. On second thought, I put the box in the hidey-hole and then locked the closet for the first time since owning the house.

Realizing the time I decided to go to bed. I felt deserted on top of Summit Ridge and an awful feeling that I would never see Jack or Carrie again.

And so ended Wednesday.

Friday, mid-morning, Charles called me at work. He was so excited I could scarcely understand him. Finally, I said, "Charles, calm down. Take a deep breath and start over."

"The house. Jack and Carrie's house. It's burning. I called the fire department and they're chugging up the hill right now. But the house is all ablaze. I saw it when I went out to put a letter in the mailbox." It sounded as though he was crying. "If I'd gone out sooner maybe—" He was crying and couldn't finish his thought.

"Charles, I'm coming home. I'll come the back way and park behind your house. I am sure the fire department will have Summit blocked." I made sure he responded before hanging up. "Duane", I took my coat off the rack. "I am going home. My neighbor just called and the Bayh house is on fire."

Duane came to his door. "Well, what can you do?" It is a valid question.

"My neighbors are quite elderly and very upset. If nothing else, I can calm them down. I'll be back." I didn't wait for his okay but got into my car and went home.

There was so much smoke. I could see it from the backside of the ridge. After I parked behind Charles house, I walked to the street. Both of the town's fire trucks were blocking the street. The house was fully engulfed. All I could think of was what would Jack have to come back to? All that was left of Carrie now was in a box in my back closet. Tears flowed down my face. Everything hit me at once. Carrie's kidnapping, Jack's testifying, the house. How much more cruel can it become? Charles and Mary were standing on their front porch watching the fire department's futile efforts to save the house. We huddled together like refugees in a strange land. Suddenly we were so alone. We had been such a close group and now it's all gone. It's a miserable feeling.

We went inside and Charles said, "I don't care if it isn't noon yet. I'm going to have a martini. Anyone care to join me?" I'm not a martini person but at that moment, it sounded like a good idea to me.

Charles got out his silver shaker and filled it partially with ice. He had once been a bartender and he didn't measure the gin as he poured it over the ice. It appeared to me that he put only half a dozen drops of vermouth in the shaker. He had martini glasses in his freezer and he filled three of them. None was left over. His measure had been sure.

He handed Mary and I each a glass. "To friends. May God guard them." I began to cry again. "Don' t you like the martini, Eleanor?" He was trying to cheer me up. And I had come home to cheer him up! We lifted out glasses and then drank. Half an hour later I said I had to get back to work. Charles offered me a mint—in case someone got close to me. "We don't want people to think you drink." That warranted a smile and I left by the front door. The fire department had put the fire out. There was very little of the house left standing. I walked to my car and returned to work.

Duane came to my office as soon as I had hung up my coat. "Phew! You smell like smoke!" Guess Charles hadn't realized that or he wouldn't have bothered with the mint.

"The Bayh house is gone, Duane. Burned almost to the ground."

Duane asked, "Was Jack home? Is he okay?"

Then I realized that he was unaware that Jack had gone to the valley in FBI custody. "Jack left with the FBI on Wednesday evening, Duane. He's testifying before a federal grand jury this week."

"Is that about Carrie's disappearance?" Duane was puzzled.

"No, it's something else altogether. In fact, the FBI thinks it may be the reason Carrie was kidnapped. Somebody didn't want Jack to testify." I didn't know how much I could, or even should, tell him.

Duane ran his hand through his hair. "By any chance, does this have anything to do with Fletcher Ellison?"

"Why would you think that, Duane?"

"Well, does it?"

I stammered for a second. "Quite honestly, Duane. I don't know. Personally, I think so. Jack thinks so. But there's no proof of any sort. I don't know."

Duane shook his head and murmured something that sounded like "That damn bastard." I feel the same way.

Late Friday evening, perhaps an hour after I had gone to bed, the telephone rang. I was going to ignore it thinking of all the "empty" calls I've gotten lately but decided maybe I should get it. I rolled over and picked up the bedroom extension. "Hello?"

"Eleanor, it's Jack. I have to talk quickly. I'm supposed to be asleep. The FBI has me nailed down pretty good. I have to testify again Monday. Did you get the box I left for you?'

I gulped. "Yes, I did. I haven't had the heart to go through it yet though."

"That's okay. Just so you have it. Do you still have the file Carrie was gathering on Ellison?"

I thought that was a strange question. "Yes. Why?"

"Well, I'm thinking it might be a good idea to get rid of it now. Send it to someone who can do something about it. We don't have to worry about Carrie's well being so let's do it."

"Jack, have you watched the news? Oh, they probably wouldn't carry Payson news anyhow. Jack, I have to tell you something."

"What's up?"

"Your house burned down this morning. The fire department thinks it was intentional."

There was a long silence. Then Jack's strained voice came back on the line. "Eleanor. Bring that file down to the capitol. Don't monkey around with taking it to the County. I have a feeling Ellison could cover up everything and anything with a couple of his fancy lies. I'll find out who you should see and leave a name or number for you at the desk here at the Hilton. Okay?"

"Okay, Jack. Whatever I can do. I'll take Monday off. And Jack—I am really sorry about the house."

"Me, too. Gotta go Eleanor. Take care of yourself this weekend." He hung up quickly but not before I heard the sobs. Maybe I shouldn't have told him. Damn! The world can be so cruel.

Chapter Twenty-Six

Monday morning I called Duane early while he was still at home. "I've got an emergency in the valley, Duane. I won't be in until later." I told him where my projects stood and assured him that everything he needed for his 11am meeting was ready and on my desk. I am glad he didn't ask what the emergency was. I am not sure I could have found words to tell him.

It's not quite a two-hour drive to Phoenix. I had a city map and had plotted a route before leaving home. Phoenix seems so large now that I am not visiting it often. Compared to Payson—actually, there's no comparison. There is a lot of traffic. Perhaps I should have waited an hour so I'd miss the morning rush hour. Too late to think about that now.

I found the Hilton and followed its parking signs to a covered garage. When I came up to the desk the clerk looked as if he had just gotten up. He looked tired but not disheveled.

"My name is Eleanor Hutchins from Payson. Did John Bayh leave a message for me?" The clerk nodded and went to a small file box behind the counter.

"You just missed Mr. Bayh. He left the hotel about ten minutes ago." He handed me a Hilton stationary envelope. My name was written in Jack's wild scrawl. I thanked the clerk and walked to the nearest chair in the lobby to sit down and read Jack's note.

"Dear Eleanor . . . I am sure we agree who torched the house. The hearing has been brutal. He's up to his eyeballs in so many things. Here's the name and phone number of the person my attorney says you should contact here in Phoenix. Take care of yourself. Watch your back. I am learning stuff I wish I never knew. He's dangerous; more than we ever thought." There was a name and number following. I looked around the lobby to find a pay phone. I crossed the lobby and stepped into a small horseshoe shaped telephone kiosk. I was waiting as the number began to ring when I saw Fletcher Ellison come in the front entrance. I put my finger on the phone to stop the ring. Then I stepped back a bit further into the kiosk. I don't think he can see me unless he is looking for me. And there's no reason he should be.

I watched as he approached the front desk, praying that the clerk wouldn't mention me. I edged out of the kiosk slightly to see him wait at the counter to be acknowledged. I couldn't see what he asked the clerk but I could read the clerk's lips when he told Fletcher that Mr. Bayh had already left the hotel.

Maybe I misread his lips but I think he actually said, "Mr. Bayh has already left the hotel." He didn't say "checked out". I'm sure of that.

Fletcher asked him something else and it looks like the clerk said, "I don't have that information." I wonder what Fletcher asked him.

Fletcher began to turn around and I shrank back into the kiosk as far as I could. I wore my brown suit so perhaps I'll blend into the background. It doesn't seem that he is scanning the lobby. He's just going back outside. When it appeared he was not coming back into the lobby, I redialed.

Three rings and the call was picked up. I explained who I was and what I wanted. The secretary put me on hold. I kept watching the front entrance. When she came back on the line she asked if I had a pen; she would give me directions on how to get to her from where I was. I fished out a pen and wrote on the note Jack had left for me. The directions seem fairly simple. Question is—can I safely go into the Hilton garage to retrieve my car without running into Fletcher. In the end, I asked the doorman if he could flag a cab for me.

The cab driver thought I was nuts when I asked him to swing through the parking garage but he did it. When I got to my car I asked him to wait and I opened my trunk and pulled out a small brown briefcase full of Carrie's gatherings from Fletcher's office.

The cabbie made some wiseass remark about not forgetting the paperwork. I told him that I had planned to drive to my destination but was a bit put off by the traffic. He nodded like he understood perfectly. "Just where is it that you want to go?" I read the address from my notes and he commented, "Yeah, if you're not into big city traffic, a cab is your best bet for the capitol."

$4.30 and less than 15 minutes, I stood in front of the Arizona State Capitol building. It's copper dome looks green in the morning sunlight. I tipped the cab driver two dollars. He pointed a half block up the street and told me I could catch a cab back to the Hilton there.

The building inside was cool and dark. I found a directory to verify where I was going. I am completely lost and can't seem to orient myself inside this domed foyer. There is a uniformed man standing near one of the staircases and I asked him how to get to the suite I wanted. He was very polite and didn't seem to think it strange that I asked directions even though he had just seen me at the directory. Official governmental buildings are so convoluted. I swear. I thanked him and went up the stairs. Even the office doors are impressive. The office lobby area looks like a designer living room in a very opulent home. A young lady, who I hadn't seen when I came in, asked if she could be of some help.

Her question startled me and I jumped. Then I laughed at myself, went to her desk and introduced myself. She asked if I would wait just a moment. She spoke so softly into the telephone that I could barely hear her. I did recognize my own name—which I suppose is natural.

In less than five minutes I was sitting across the desk from the State Attorney. I handed him the files Carrie had entrusted to me and explained what she thought and believed and what she actually knew. He asked why she hadn't brought these documents in herself. My breath seemed to clog my throat and, for a moment, I could not reply.

I told him the story of the last week and a half; right down to Jack's leaving the note for me.

He went through the documents one by one. Carrie had put a note on each document explaining why she doubted it. He took a yellow pad out of a desk drawer and began writing notes. An hour later he stopped and said, "Fortunately, even without your friend to corroborate these alleged forgeries, there's enough here for us to proceed."

I stood up to leave and he asked if I needed to have my parking validated. I told him I had taken a cab from the Hilton and why. He shook his head. "I have no doubt why you're paranoid; all I can say is please be very careful. Before you leave, I'd like your address and phone number there in Payson." He handed me a notepad and I printed my name, address and telephone number. "If you run into any trouble, call me." He handed me his business card.

Once I got into the hallway, I slipped his business card under my driver's license. Yes, I am hiding it. I am truly afraid of Fletcher now.

On the sidewalk I oriented myself to where the cab had dropped me so I could find where to catch another. I stopped by a small sign and within half a minute a cab pulled up. I opened the door and got in. "Hilton Downtown, please." Strange, it cost $4.90 for the trip back. I only tipped a dollar.

Two hours later I was at my office in Payson. I waved at Duane as I went into my office. On my desk sat a small vase with three beautiful white roses. The card read, "Now that you have no neighbors, perhaps you'll reconsider having dinner with me. How about this evening? Fletcher." Incredible!

Chapter Twenty-Seven

The drive down and back had been arduous and I was tired. It was lunch time in Payson. Duane asked if I wanted to take lunch and I told him that I was too tired to get up again. Then he asked why I had come into the office—"You could have just called me from home."

"Duane, I have things to do today. I had to go to the valley on something very important but I have three escrows to review and type for tomorrow." He shook his head and then asked if he could bring back something to eat at my desk. That sounded like a good idea. "Anything will do." I hadn't put my purse away yet. I pulled $5 out and handed it to him. "I'm not picky."

Duane laughed at that, put the money in his pocket, put on his coat and went out the back door. For some reason he's been parking behind the office lately. If I think of it later, I'll ask him why. Usually he likes clients to know he's in. I pulled my rolling file next to the desk and extracted the three folders I need to work on.

By the time Duane returned, I was hungry. He had brought a roast beef on wheat. He laid the change on my desk pad. "I think I remember that you like wheat bread." I said I did. "Great. Get some coffee and eat. Nothing's so important it can't wait fifteen minutes." I smiled. He tries to be so gruff and can never pull it off.

About an hour later, Fletcher called. Duane had picked up the phone for some reason. "Fletcher, I've got Eleanor's nose to the grindstone. No way can she talk to you now. Can I take a message?" Duane was listening. "No, I know for fact she cannot have dinner with you this evening. She's doing some research for me that I need in the morning." He was listening again. "Of course, if you want to hear it from Eleanor, I'll transfer the call to her." He was listening. "That's okay Fletcher. Some of us in town have to work for a living." He hung up.

Duane came into my office. "Did you hear all that?" I nodded. "Perhaps I overstepped my bounds—maybe you want to have dinner with him? You're down to three roses."

I smiled and said, "I don't care if we're down to no roses. I don't want to have dinner with that man." Duane laughed and left me to finish my escrow packages. Suddenly, I wasn't as tired as I had been.

I finished my day's work just an hour after I would normally have left the office. In other words, I must be goofing off most days if I can come in at 12:30 and still get the work completed almost on schedule. I think I won't mention that to Duane. He said he had work to catch up on and is still in the office now at 6.

Just as I was putting things back into my rolling file, Duane came to my door. "Ready to call it a day?" I admitted I was.

"Gosh, Fletcher is really going to believe me now. I have your nose so much to the grindstone that you had to work overtime. Want me to follow you home?"

"Do you think that's necessary?" I picked up my purse and sat it on my desk. "Shouldn't he be across the street by now?"

"Should and is are two different verbs, Eleanor. Personally, I don't trust the man to do anything he should do." Duane put on his coat. "I don't see his truck in front of his office or across the street. I'll follow you home."

Not knowing where Fletcher was made me uneasy. I am not sure why. The man is such a snake. I am so sure he had something to do with Carrie's disappearance and Jack and Carrie's house burning down. What else is he capable of doing? I don't really want to know. I put on my coat, picked up my purse and said, "Okay, mighty leader, let's go."

Duane smiled and locked the office behind us.

We followed Wade Lane to the Ridge—that's the back way in. As I crested Summit Ridge I looked down onto Main Street and McLean. I didn't realize what a view was available from this point on the street. I pulled over and Duane came up next to me.

"What's wrong?" He rolled down his window and called to me.

"Look down at the Winchester."

He did. "Do you want to go home or turn around and go somewhere else?" Fletcher's truck was parked at the Winchester. From the saloon my house is in the direct line of sight. He was waiting for me to come home. I just know it.

"No, I'll go on home. But I think I'll put the car in the garage and not turn on any lights in the back of the house." My driveway was shielded from view by a small stand of poplar trees and a shaggy old fir. I could get in without being seen if I go in the front door.

Duane wasn't so sure. "After everything that's happened, are you sure you'll be okay?"

"Duane, I can't be sure of anything. But if I don't answer the door or the phone, he'll not know I'm home." I pulled back on the street and continued down the ridge.

After I had put the car in the garage, Duane said, "I want you to call me at home at 8 and at 10. If I don't hear from you, I'm calling the police."

This shook me. "Duane, do you know something I don't? You're scaring me." Suddenly chilled, I wrapped my arms around my self.

"No. I believe you know everything I know except that I know Fletcher better than you do. He's a devious, unstable man." He got back into his car. "Call me at 8 and at 10." He rolled up his window and drove back the way we had come. I went into the house.

Something felt wrong to me the minute I entered. Turning on the living room lights I realized that the room had been ransacked. I went to my bedroom—it was in even greater disarray. I called the police. A patrol car must have been close by as just a minute or two later, an officer was at the front door. Right behind him was my boss, Duane.

"I was nearly back to the highway when the patrol car passed me at a pretty good clip. On impulse I followed him. What's up?" Duane had his arm around me like a father trying to coax his child out of crying.

The officer asked when I had last been in the house. "About 6am this morning." He wanted to know if I was sure of the time.

Duane spoke up. "Eleanor called me at 6 this morning saying she was leaving the house then."

"And you haven't been back all day?" The officer was being petty.

"No, I had business out of town and went straight to the office when I returned. I am just now coming home." The chill in my bones was deepening.

"Is there anything missing?" The officer began walking down the hallway toward my bedroom. "Have you checked all the rooms?"

I admitted I had not. The living room and my bedroom were definitely disturbed and I called without checking further.

"Would you mind checking the other rooms of the house?" The officer stood at my bedroom door. Closet doors were open; drawers pulled half out or dumped on the floor. Even the medicine chest in my bathroom had been opened. The closets in the two spare bedrooms were open and contents laying about. The hidey hole was undisturbed. My knitting file cabinet in the back bedroom was a total wreck. The drawers were out; all the pattern files were scattered across the bed.

My mind suddenly flashed. My god, if I hadn't taken the file down to the valley this morning, he would have found it. I looked at Duane and felt like a deer standing in the headlights. He crossed the room quickly and asked, "Are you okay?"

I stepped away from the officer and whispered to Duane. "It had to have been Fletcher. He was looking for something. How he knew Carrie had a file on him, I don't know. And why he thought I had it, I don't know. Unless he ransacked the Bayh house before he torched it. If I hadn't gone down this morning, he would have found it."

Duane looked at me sort of dazed. "What are you babbling about, Eleanor? Where did you go this morning?"

"Wait. I'll tell you in a minute." I continued looking through my scrambled home. I could not see that anything was missing.

The police officer asked, "Well, is anything gone?"

"It's hard to tell with everything in such disarray but I don't think so." I was doubly distressed because he had turned on all the lights in the house. Now Fletcher would know I was home.

At that moment, the telephone rang. I expected the caller would hang up but answered it anyway. Surprise! It was Fletcher. "Have you changed your mind about dinner?"

"No, Mr. Ellison. I have not changed my mind about dinner. I really need to clean my house tonight." I hung up.

The officer got out a pad and pen and suggested I sit on the couch. Duane called home and said he'd be a few minutes late; he'd explain when he got there. He sat in a chair close to the officer.

The officer re-asked when I had last been home; when did I get home; was anything missing? He wrote everything down. When he had finished he stood up and said, "Unless you have an idea who may have done this, there's not much more I can do than take a report."

I acknowledged that and said, "Let me think on it. Maybe someone or something will come to mind." He accepted that answer, shook hands with Duane and left.

As soon as he was out the door, Duane said, "Okay Eleanor. What's really going on here? Where did you go this morning?"

It took me more than half hour to tell him everything. He was stunned. "You actually believe that stuff we've had filed for him was forged? I knew the man was crooked but this is unbelievable."

"Carrie knew something more than just the forgeries, I think. And I believe that Fletcher was responsible for her disappearance. And for their house being burned and for Jack being called to a federal grand jury. Fletcher is up to his neck in something no good and we're all going to pay for it if we can't stop him."

"What did the state attorney say this morning?" Duane was agitated beyond anything I'd seen before. Now he was pacing. "My god, could we be implicated in this? How would we know we were filing forgeries?"

I could see that Duane's agitation was more for what could happen to his, and the title company's, reputation than how crooked Fletcher was.

"Duane, I am quite sure the company will be okay. We never prepared any of those documents. We just sent them with our courier to the County Clerk. Don't worry about reputation at a time like this. I think we have a bigger problem on our hands."

Duane sat down and nodded. "Of course, you're right. I am finding it so hard to imagine what a rotten, dirty, scumbag Fletcher really is."

He got up, ready to leave again. "Are you going to be okay here tonight?"

"Of course, I am. Fletcher didn't find what he was looking for. He's sure I don't have it . . . whatever he thinks it is." I finally took off my coat and hung it in the hall closet. It was the only thing hanging; everything else was on the closet floor. "And besides, I have George's gun."

A thought struck me. Do I have George's gun? I didn't see it when looking through the rubble of my bedroom. I ran down the hallway. Duane was right behind me. The nightstand drawer was hanging, like a brown tongue, out of the stand. There was no gun!

"Duane, he's taken George's gun!" I totally panicked.

"Call the police and tell them you've found something missing. Can you identify it?" Duane picked up the bedroom extension, dialed the number and handed me the receiver.

Chapter Twenty-Eight

Over the next few weeks I ran into Fletcher Ellison twice. Both times I felt he had planned to accidentally run into me. He was most cordial; sickeningly so. I tried to not see him but he was so blatant I had to recognize him. Both times he inquired as to my state of health, how was my job and would I reconsider and have dinner with him. Each time I said, "Fine. Great. No." He told me I was being flippant and rude. And I told him that I was not interested in anything but a business relationship with him. He acted quite miffed but walked away from me without further urging.

Thanksgiving came and went and Christmas was looming before I ran into Fletcher again. I was in the J.C. Penney catalogue store looking for a particular color yarn in their general catalogue. Fletcher walked into the store and came directly to me. "I've chased you all over town today."

"What?" I wasn't sure I had heard him correctly. "You've been chasing me?"

He cleared this throat. "Well, Christmas is coming and I wondered if you would knit a shawl for me. I haven't been able to find anything suitable for my mother. I know you have a large collection of patterns and thought perhaps you would be amiable to helping out an old friend."

I stood very still. He was admitting he has seen my pattern collection. Did he realize what he had just said?

"I'm sorry, Mr. Ellison. I just don't have time to knit anything extra this year." This was a true statement but definitely not the reason I didn't want to knit for him.

"Oh, well, do you have any suggestions?"

I had just flipped through the Christmas catalogue a few minutes before and had seen sweaters, stoles and shawls. "The J.C. Penney catalogue has some beautiful things this Christmas. Perhaps you should check it out." I handed him the catalogue.

He stood there unspeaking. I believe he had not expected this response. I can't imagine what he did expect but this wasn't it. He took the catalogue and went to another counter. I decided that the color yarn I wanted wasn't available and left the store. Maybe Basha's would have the color. For a grocery store, they had a wide variety of dry goods and frequently carried yarn.

A few days before Christmas, Duane took us all to his annual office Christmas dinner. We went to Mario's, the small Italian restaurant at the south entrance to town. As we were leaving, Fletcher came into the dining room. "Duane, when are you going to invite me to one of these shindigs?"

Duane was standing holding his wife's coat. "As soon as you're an employee." His wife slipped into her coat.

Fletcher had a crestfallen look and said, "Aw, come on. I bring you plenty of business. I'm like a member of your staff already."

"Next thing you know, you'll be wanting a paycheck twice a month.' Duane proceeded to put on his own coat. "Don't you take your staff to Christmas dinner?"

"Staff? What staff? I don't have a staff anymore and haven't had for a couple months. You know that." Fletcher was getting a bit red faced and all of us, except Duane and wife, began to ease away from the table. Jimmy had brought a date this year and Cyndi had a new boyfriend. I was the only single person there and I moved the quickest. Jimmy and his girlfriend followed behind me as close as a shadow on a sunny day. If Fletcher was going into another of his tirade's, he wouldn't have much of an audience.

Bless Duane. He stalled Fletcher long enough that we were all able to get in our vehicles and leave. Jimmy followed me home and I invited he and Kathy, his girlfriend, in for a nightcap. Kathy is fairly new to Payson and asked, "What was that all about? Who is this guy?"

Jimmy grinned and looked at his watch. "I'm not sure you want to stay up that late to hear the whole story." He went on to tell her about the dinner last year. He also mentioned that Fletcher was an attorney in town whose secretary disappeared in October and her husband vanished shortly after his house burned a few weeks later.

We all believe that Jack is in some sort of witness protection program but Jimmy didn't tell her that. He really made Fletcher out to be the town bad guy. And, thinking about it, that's not too great an exaggeration.

They stayed for nearly an hour. I won't be surprised if they announce an engagement some day soon. I asked Jimmy if he is still living where I could see his house and he could see mine. He is. Somehow that is comforting. I reminded him he was to come up quickly if he ever saw my red flag. He said he hadn't forgotten. Poor Kathy looked at us as though we were lunatics.

The following Monday I received two exquisite roses in a bud vase. All the card said was, "Merry Christmas. Fletcher"

The last ten days of 1981 flew by. My parents came up for Christmas and I went to their house for New Year's. My brothers were home for the holiday as well and we had some great remembrance discussions. Being home was a good feeling. The old song "There's No Place Like Home for the Holidays" seem to come to mind to us at the same time and we sang the entire song—twice. My dad seemed quite pleased. My mother hid a tear or two. It's difficult to explain New Year's Day. It was comforting and disturbing at the same time. But it was good to be together again. It was better to be out of Payson.

Chapter Twenty-Nine

January was more than half over when Fletcher put up a sign in his office window that said the office would be closed for two weeks. He was seen driving south out of town in his large pickup.

When he returned, he spent a great deal of time in his office. More than we had seen since late summer last year. Duane said he never saw any clients go in or out of the office though. Fletcher's sudden industry was a puzzle.

Meanwhile, in January, I had received two telephone calls from the State Attorney's office. They had been doing research on the documents Carrie had gathered. As Carrie was unavailable, they asked that I make myself available when the time came to bring Fletcher before a grand jury. There were charges of forgery, grand larceny, and a couple other things that went over my head. I told them I would make myself available but wouldn't my testimony be hearsay? No, Carrie had given me the documents—that's all my testimony would cover. Something about chain of evidence, or possession, or something—I don't know exactly what.

The assistant attorney I spoke with said that the grand jury would not convene soon on this matter but they wanted assurances I would testify without subpoena.

As summer started Fletcher was in his office less and less. We all wondered how he was living. He could not possibly have legal income. One afternoon in late August, I ran into Jerry White, from the lumber mill, at the Knotty Pine Café. He mentioned that he had been in National City and San Diego setting up new sales offices there. I said that sounded exciting. He told me they were marketing log cabin style pre-fab homes and thought San Diego County was a good market.

He talked for quite a while and then mentioned he had run into Fletcher Ellison in National City a month or so ago and had gone with him to a party. He met a nice girl and hoped to be able to continue the relationship. Fletcher had told Jerry he's down there pretty frequently. "He said anytime I wanted to come down for a weekend, we could work out something." He added, "I think Fletcher has found a girl as well. Her name is Chris Shafer and she happens to live with the girl I'm nuts about."

When I got into the office Monday I mentioned this to Duane. "Could he be so besot by a woman that'd he'd neglect his practice?"

Duane didn't think so. He said, "There has to be something else going on. I can't see Fletcher letting his practice slide for a romantic interlude. He thinks he's a lady's man but that would be over the top even for Fletcher."

"By the way," Duane added. "How many roses are you down to now?"

I laughed. "The last was two. But San Diego has kept him busy for 6 or seven months now. I think I may be out of the loop."

"Oh, that's too bad." Duane was being a smart ass.

A week later the town was buzzing. Rumor had it that Fletcher Ellison had been shot and killed in National City. No one seemed to know what the truth was or what had happened. The FBI was at Jerry's house about 4am one morning and by the time the rest of us were up and at work, Jerry had left for National City. It was quite a few days before he came back to Payson and informed us that the FBI thinks that Chris Shafer is actually Carrie Bayh.

It's an understatement to say we are stunned. As the days went by we learned that Chris Shafer was Carrie Bayh—she had been left in the desert for dead after she disappeared from Payson. She is suffering with amnesia and doesn't remember Payson or any of us at all. I am devastated. I am elated. My best friend is alive but she doesn't have any memory of me. How can this be?

I talked with Jerry and asked if he thought I could go down to see Carrie. He didn't know if it'd be a good idea. But he would ask her roommate, Sally Reed, what she thought. He also plans to ask Sally Reed, to marry him once things were settled down a bit. Sally is a nurse and he's hoping she'll not only marry him but also agree to live with him in Payson.

Of course, none of us can grasp the idea that Carrie isn't dead and Fletcher Ellison is.

Chapter Thirty

Almost before I knew it, October was upon us. It is a sad time. It has been a year since I last saw Jack and Carrie Bayh. Even though I know now that Carrie is alive and so is Jack, somewhere, it's a struggle to accept everything that has happened. It's been a tumultuous year.

A month or so after the fire that burned the Bayh house to the ground, Carrie's folks came up and contracted with a company to clear the rubble away. The lot was soon bare. I had never seen it like that before. The apple and pear trees that Jack had planted are flourishing and the azaleas on the back slope are still green. These were the only reminders left in Payson of two great people. I keep hoping that Jack will hear of Fletcher's death and leave the witness protection program. I guess there's little hope of that happening. Do people ever leave witness protection?

The same week the ashes were covered with gravel, I scanned the Multiple Listings in the paper and saw that Ron and Donna's house is up for sale. I guess they think they'll never feel the same way about Payson as they had so short a time ago. Everything's changed. Everything is slightly off kilter.

I had a couple days of total melancholy. Duane suggested I take some time off. It was the afternoon of one of those days that the FBI knocked on my front door. They asked if they could come in. What do you say to the FBI—no? Not hardly. I invited them in.

One agent took a revolver out of his briefcase. "Do you recognize this weapon?" He handed it to me.

I turned it over and looked at it carefully. It looked like George's gun. I looked on the bottom of the grip. It was George's gun. In tiny little letters he had carved his initials on the grip the day he brought the gun home. Those two little letters looked a foot high at the moment. GH.

"Yes, I recognize this gun." I handed it back to the agent. "How did you get it?"

The agent asked, "When did you last see this weapon?"

I knew when I had last not seen it. When had I actually last seen it? "I am not sure when I last saw it but I knew it was gone after my house had been burglarized and ransacked last year. I reported it to the local police department."

They looked at each other. "We know. We just wanted you to identify the weapon as yours."

"When or how did you get it?' I was confused. I thought Fletcher had taken the gun. How did the FBI end up with it?

"We recovered it from the body of Fletcher Ellison after a shoot out a few weeks ago in National City." They paused there. I wanted to say—and? I waited for them to continue. They just sat there.

Finally, I said, "I always suspected he was the one who had broken into my house. I guess this is proof." They sort of nodded. Not a real 'you're right' nod. Just a nod. "Will I ever be able to get it back? It was my late husband's gun."

"As soon as the investigation is completed we can return the weapon to you." Completed? Isn't Fletcher dead? What else has to be done? Dead is dead for goodness sakes.

"Thank you very much. I would appreciate it." I didn't know what else to say. These guys weren't into conversation or even small talk.

They asked me to sign a document acknowledging ownership of the gun and requesting return of same when the case was concluded. Then they were gone. Damn. The FBI can be so frustrating.

Chapter Thirty-One

February 6, 1983—Carrie Bayh is back in town. She looks wonderful; she sounds wonderful; she doesn't remember any of us. Her friend Sally Reed and Jerry (from the lumber mill) bought a house a month or so ago. And their wedding is here in Payson next week. I understand Sally is going to work at Pyle Memorial Hospital—at least, that's the rumor.

Carrie met with some of us this afternoon for drinks and conversation. We all agreed to call her Chris as that is the only name she knows for herself. Her story of kidnap and recovery scares me badly. Fletcher Ellison was worse than I could ever imagine. And, the most ironic part, she told about his trying to woo her and the white roses he sent to her, one less each time. My dear friend Carrie. She didn't give in either. She was afraid of him though she couldn't pin down any reason. She met him at a dance she had attended with her roommate, Sally.

Carrie looks the same, she sounds the same but she doesn't remember me at all. She did say she could imagine we had been friends. But she's somebody else now—amnesia is a terrible thing to suffer. She said that she was in a coma for three months and since then has only had glimpses of her former life. I asked her what became of Jack. She said that she had been told that he was in the Witness Protection Program but didn't know anything else. And, she said, perhaps that was fortunate as she doesn't remember him either. Fletcher surely took a toll on that couple.

The FBI shot and killed Fletcher but that doesn't help any of us at all. We are now aware that he was up to more trouble than we could ever know. That he'd been trafficking drugs and thought Carrie would remember who she was and what he was. That had to be the greatest crime of all. He thought he had to kill her. Fortunately, even though Carrie is now Chris Shaffer, she is still an intelligent woman who managed to foil Fletcher's efforts to kill her off. She must have sensed his evilness. Why else would she have been so wary of him?

Home alone now I am wondering how many roses Carrie, Chris, had gotten from Fletcher? The local florist told me once that no one but me ever resisted him to the very last rose. He said I was the only one who refused to be drawn into his web . . . a web of lies and deceit. It's comforting to know that the woman who had been my best friend never gave in to his 'charms' either. Perhaps some hidden memory kept her from succumbing to his advances. Unconsciously she knew he was dangerous.

Fletcher Ellison always believed he was a suave, debonair, handsome and witty man. He went through life telling wild and, often, humorous stories. This time the laugh was on him.

###

Printed in the United States
68310LVS00005B